Big Secret or Big Trouble!

Creeping as noiselessly as the Indians in Crying Moon's story, the girls moved toward the cabin. The door creaked open. Clasping hands, Jessica, Elizabeth, and Amy stepped silently into the inky blackness. As their eyes adjusted to the light, the girls could see that they were in a small room.

"There's nothing here," Elizabeth said nervously. "Let's go back now."

"Do you think we should see what's in the next room?" Jessica asked, peering toward it.

"No!" Amy and Elizabeth said.

"All right," Jessica agreed, "let's get out of here."

The girls turned, eager to make their escape, when suddenly a bright light appeared on the front door.

"What's that?" Jessica said, her voice quavering.

Then Elizabeth screamed. Outlined against the yellow glow was a huge dark shadow, blocking their way to safety. For a few seconds the girls stood there, paralyzed. Then, with screams and shrieks, they flew out the door and ran down the hill.

Bantam Books in the SWEET VALLEY TWINS series
Ask your bookseller for the books you have missed

Sweet Valley Twins Super Editions

SWEET VALLEY TWINS
◇ SUPER EDITION ◇

The Big Camp Secret

◇

Written by
Jamie Suzanne

Created by
FRANCINE PASCAL

A BANTAM SKYLARK BOOK®
NEW YORK · TORONTO · LONDON · SYDNEY · AUCKLAND

THE BIG CAMP SECRET
A BANTAM BOOK 0 553 400142

Originally published in U.S.A. by
Bantam Skylark Books

First publication in Great Britain

PRINTING HISTORY
Bantam edition published 1989

Sweet Vally High® and Sweet Valley Twins
are registered trademarks of Francine Pascal.
Conceived by Francine Pascal.
Produced by Daniel Weiss Associates, Inc.,
27 West 29th Street, New York NY 10011.
Cover art by James Mathewuse.
All rights reserved.

Bantam Books are published by Transworld Publishers Ltd.,
61–63 Uxbridge Road, Ealing, London W5 5SA, in Australia by
Transworld Publishers (Australia) Pty. Ltd., 15–23 Helles
Avenue, Moorebank, NSW 2170, and in New Zealand by
Transworld Publishers (N.Z.) Ltd., Cnr. Moselle and Waipareira
Avenues, Henderson, Auckland.

Printed and bound in Great Britain by
Cox & Wyman Ltd., Reading, Berks.

The Big Camp Secret

One

◇

"Just think, by this time tomorrow, we'll be at Lake Loconda," Jessica Wakefield exclaimed, her blue-green eyes sparkling. "It's going to be wonderful!"

"The greatest camp ever," her twin sister Elizabeth agreed.

Elizabeth's best friend, Amy Sutton, nodded enthusiastically. Only Grace Oliver sat quietly, her eyes down.

The girls were drinking milk shakes at Casey's. Elizabeth and Jessica had come to the Sweet Valley Mall to buy new shorts and T-shirts for sleepaway camp when they ran into Amy and Grace. Now, as they all sat in the ice cream parlor, the conversation turned to the fun in store for the next two weeks.

"I'll be able to go horseback riding every day," Elizabeth said.

"Don't forget the campfires," Amy added. "And arts and crafts, treasure hunts . . ."

Jessica laughed. "Amy, you sound like the camp brochure."

"I can't help it. I wish we were leaving today."

"Me, too," Jessica said. "But tomorrow's not too far away, especially since we're leaving so early in the morning."

Elizabeth couldn't help noticing Grace's sad expression.

"Grace," she asked gently, "are you all right? You don't seem very excited about camp. You *are* coming, aren't you?"

"I . . . I thought I was," Grace said, nervously playing with a strand of her red hair.

"Thought?" Amy asked.

"Well, it's just that I'm not going after all," Grace said, her cheeks getting flushed.

Elizabeth and Jessica exchanged surprised looks.

"But why not?" Jessica asked bluntly.

"Well, I . . . oh, look here come Lila and Ellen," Grace said, visibly relieved at the interruption.

Jessica turned to wave at her friends. "More Unicorns for Camp Loconda," she said with satisfaction.

Elizabeth frowned. She and Jessica were identical twins. Both had long blond hair, blue-green eyes, and matching dimples in their left cheeks—but their personalities were as different as their looks were identical. Elizabeth, who was four minutes older, often thought of herself as the big sister. She was the more serious one who liked working hard in school, spending time with her friends, and sometimes just being alone to read a good book. She was also an editor on the sixth-grade newspaper, *The Sweet Valley Sixers* and hoped to become a professional writer some day. Jessica was more inclined to just have a good time and do as little work in school as she could get away with. She preferred to spend most of her time with the Unicorns, an exclusive group of the prettiest and most popular girls at Sweet Valley Middle School. Jessica was very proud to be a member, although Elizabeth didn't think much of the group. She frequently referred to the girls as the Snob Squad because they spent most of their time gossiping about boys, fashions, and movie stars. Lila Fowler, the daughter of one of the wealthier men in Sweet Valley, and Jessica's best friend, was one of the worst.

With Ellen Riteman right behind her, Lila Fowler marched up to their table with a satisfied smile on her face and said, "Guess what? I'm not going to camp."

"Why not?" Jessica demanded.

"Because I'm going to Paris with my grandmother instead."

Paris! Jessica couldn't believe it. No matter what anyone else was doing, Lila always seemed to go one better. "When did that happen?" she asked, trying to keep her voice even.

"This morning," Lila said gaily. "Grandma is going to visit some friends and she wants me to come along. We may stop in London, too. Just think, I'll see the Eiffel Tower, the changing of the guard at Buckingham Palace. Doesn't it sound wonderful?"

"Wonderful," Jessica said glumly.

"I guess that leaves an extra bed in our bunk," Ellen said.

A number of the girls from Sweet Valley had been assigned to Bunk Seven, including the twins, Amy Sutton, and Ellen.

Lila shrugged. "Well, don't miss me *too* much." She glanced at her bright red watch. "I have to go pick up my new passport. I'll call you later, Jessica, and give you all the details."

Before Jessica could say anything, Lila walked out of Casey's and faded into the crowd of shoppers.

Elizabeth knew Jessica was feeling a little jealous. "Oh, who cares about Paris?" she said. "Camp is going to be more fun than wandering around a foreign city."

Jessica started to smile. "Right. Paris doesn't have a camp full of boys right across the lake."

"Boys that include Ken Matthews and Bruce Patman," Ellen added significantly.

"We won't be seeing much of them, though," Elizabeth said. "The camps are separate."

"Oh, I don't know," Jessica said thoughtfully. "It shouldn't be too hard to get together with the boys."

"What do you have in mind?" Ellen asked with interest.

Jessica shrugged. "Nothing. Yet."

"There're going to be plenty of other things to keep us busy," Elizabeth said, ignoring her sister. She didn't think that boys were necessary for a good time.

"I'm looking forward to the canoe trips," Amy said.

Jessica grinned. "I guess Lila won't be the only one having a great time."

Grace, who had been sitting quietly, now got up abruptly. "I have to get home."

"How come?" Amy wanted to know. "It's still early."

"I just do." Grace's voice was shaky. She dashed out before anyone could question her further.

"What's with her?" Jessica frowned.

"We probably upset her. Here we are talking about all the great things we're going to do after she just told us she can't go," Amy said.

"Why isn't she going?" Ellen asked.

"I don't know, but I'm going to see if I can catch up to her," Elizabeth said with concern. "She seems pretty upset."

Elizabeth hurried through the crowd of Saturday shoppers until she caught up with Grace. "Hey, wait up," she said, putting her hand on Grace's shoulder.

Grace brushed away the tears that had been falling down her cheeks. "What is it, Elizabeth?"

Elizabeth led her outside, toward a stone bench. "Let's sit down."

"I really have to get home."

"C'mon, you can sit down for a minute and talk to me."

Grace knew she was trapped. "All right," she said, taking a seat on the bench.

Elizabeth handed her a tissue and Grace dabbed at her eyes. "Now tell me, why can't you go to camp?" Elizabeth asked gently.

"It's my parents," Grace said softly. "They're thinking of getting a divorce. They haven't decided for sure, but they fight all the time."

"That's awful," Elizabeth said sympathetically.

"They're taking separate vacations to think things over and they want me to stay at my godmother Kay's house while they're gone."

"While the rest of us are at Camp Loconda," Elizabeth said as she began to understand Grace's dilemma.

"That's right." Grace sniffed. "I'll miss all the fun."

"But I thought you were set to go to camp."

"We had decided on it, but then my parents changed their minds. I think they want me to be with family."

"Do you like Kay?" Elizabeth asked.

"Oh, Kay's great, but I'd much rather be going to camp with the rest of you. I've been looking forward to it for weeks."

Elizabeth thought for a moment. "Couldn't you just tell your parents that?"

Grace shook her head. "They're so tense about everything. I don't want to cause any trouble. It might start another fight and if it does. . . ."

"You're afraid they might really get angry at each other and decide the divorce is a good idea," Elizabeth finished for her.

"They're so close to doing it already," Grace said sadly. "One more fight and . . ." Grace's voice trailed off.

"But Grace, if they knew how much you wanted to go to camp, they might let you."

A hopeful expression came into Grace's green eyes. "Do you think so?"

"Well, you can try to bring it up," Elizabeth said. "Just be diplomatic. Isn't it worth giving it one more shot?"

For the first time in a long while, Grace felt hopeful. "You're right. It's worth another try." She rose to her feet, a determined look on her face. "I'll go home and ask them right now."

"Great," Elizabeth said, smiling. "I'll keep

my fingers crossed and maybe I'll see you on the bus tomorrow, heading for Lake Loconda."

"I hope so," Grace said.

It wasn't a long walk from the mall to her house, but Grace walked as slowly as she possibly could. Her determination to bring up the subject of camp was fading quickly. Going home was always unpleasant lately. Grace sighed. She didn't know why her parents fought all the time. Not long ago they had been a happy family. But then her father, who was an accountant, started working late almost every night, and the arguing had begun. After that, her parents seemed to find all kinds of things to disagree about. Sometimes Grace went to her room and played her radio loudly so she wouldn't have to hear the harsh words, but she couldn't ignore the tense feelings and the unhappy looks.

Then, a couple of weeks ago, her parents sat down with her and told her they were thinking of getting a divorce. It was the worst moment of Grace's life. Yet, no matter how much she cried and how often she protested, her parents wouldn't change their minds.

Her father was going on a fishing trip, and

her mother was going to a fancy spa up the California coast. Each would have time to think before making a final decision. But from what Grace had seen, she didn't have much hope that they'd stay together. She was almost certain her parents would go through with the divorce, and she dreaded it.

Grace headed through her pretty front yard toward the front door. Before she was halfway up the walk she could hear loud voices coming from inside.

"Well, I'm sorry you feel that way," Mrs. Oliver was saying, "but this has been very hard on me."

"It's been hard on all of us. I just hope that we make the right decision about what we're going to do with the rest of our lives. A lot of people will be affected by our decision."

Grace wished she could turn and run in the other direction, but she knew she had no choice. She marched to the door, turned the handle, and went inside.

"Oh, Grace, I'm glad you're home," her mother called. "Come into the living room."

Grace looked unhappily at her mother and father. They both had tight, hard looks on their faces.

"Hi," she said quietly.

"You have to pack," her mother said brusquely. "I don't want to rush around at the last minute."

Grace knew this was the time to speak up about camp, but before she could, Mr. Oliver said, "Oh, leave her alone, Lauren. I'm sure Grace knows she has to get ready."

"I'm just reminding her," Mrs. Oliver snapped. "Kay is doing us a big favor by taking Grace and I don't want her having to buy things because we forgot to pack them."

"I appreciate everything Kay is doing for us, but all you had to do was make a list. You're always so disorganized."

"Me? What are you talking about? Who forgot his passport the last time we went away?"

Mr. Oliver's face grew red. "I wouldn't have forgotten it if you had left it where it was supposed to be. And I might remind you, it was you who forgot our. . . ."

Grace turned and tiptoed out of the room. Her parents didn't notice.

"Dad, are the hamburgers ready yet?" Elizabeth stopped beside the grill on their patio, where her father stood flipping burgers. He was wearing his Father's Day gift from the twins, a bright red apron that read, "I'm the Cook."

"This isn't a fast food restaurant," Mr. Wakefield said with a grin. "Sometimes you have to wait for perfection."

"Give me quantity, not quality," Steven Wakefield answered from the pool, where he was splashing around.

Fourteen-year-old Steven looked like a younger version of his dad, tall and dark. Sometimes he was a great brother, but most of the time he was as obnoxious as he could be, right down to his annoying eating habits. The family joke was that Steven would eat anything that didn't eat him first.

The Wakefields had decided to have a farewell barbecue for the twins on their last night at home. Elizabeth was setting out paper plates and plastic utensils on the picnic table, and her mother was in the house making a salad. Jessica, as was often the case when there was work to be done, was nowhere to be found. Sometimes it bothered Elizabeth that she got stuck with so many of the chores, but in many ways it was easier to do them herself than quarrel with Jessica about whose turn it was to load the dishwasher or clear the table.

"Dad, did you ever go to sleepaway camp?" Elizabeth asked as she arranged the forks and knives.

"As a matter of fact, I did." A dreamy expression crossed his face. "I was on the all-star baseball team one year. And another time I took the swimming championship."

"That's great, Dad."

"We also hid our counselor's clothes one year," Mr. Wakefield said with a smile.

"You didn't!"

"Every day we took one item from his duffel bag. By the time camp ended, he barely had enough to wear home."

Elizabeth laughed. "That was a terrible thing to do."

"It was," he admitted. "But that was one of the things that made the summer so much fun. Although, I do have to admit, I was very homesick my first year."

"You, homesick?" Elizabeth couldn't have been more surprised. Her father always seemed so fearless. Then a horrible thought struck Elizabeth.

"You don't think I'll be homesick, do you?"

Mr. Wakefield looked up from the grill. "Now don't let that scare you. You've been away from home before, but I never had. If you do feel a twinge of homesickness, do what helped me."

"What was that?" Elizabeth asked with interest.

"I would allow myself to think about my family for five minutes, but no longer. Then I would make myself start having fun again."

"I'll remember that," Elizabeth said thoughtfully.

Just as Elizabeth finished setting out the ketchup, mustard, and cola, Jessica reappeared.

"Good timing," Elizabeth said pointedly.

"I was busy," Jessica informed her, stealing a potato chip from the large plastic bowl in the middle of the table.

"Doing what?" Elizabeth stopped what she was doing to look at Jessica, who had her "I have a plan" expression on her face. From experience, Elizabeth knew Jessica's plans almost always led to trouble.

Jessica pulled her to one side. "Lizzie, doesn't it seem like a shame to have all the boys of Camp Running Bear on the other side of Lake Loconda, where we can't even see them?"

Elizabeth shrugged. "That's just the way camp is, Jess. We can't do anything about it." She turned to go into the kitchen, but Jessica stopped her.

"That's not a very good answer, Liz. I think being with just girls for two whole weeks might get boring."

"Jess, just this afternoon you were telling me how exciting camp was going to be."

"I know. It just seems like a waste to have the boys so close by."

"Jessica Wakefield, you're not thinking of planning a trip to the boys' camp, are you?"

Jessica tried to look shocked. "Me?"

"Yes, you."

"Well, I've got to think of something. I just got off the phone with Lila and all she could talk about was how great Paris was going to be." Jessica pouted. "She said she'd probably come home with a French boyfriend."

"I doubt that. She doesn't even speak French."

"The only thing that'll make her jealous is if I have a fabulous time at camp," Jessica said desperately.

"But you will, Jess. Just think of all the great activities at Camp Loconda."

"Oh, the activities are going to be fun, but

they won't impress Lila. No, it's got to be something much more spectacular than that."

Elizabeth folded her arms in front of her. "I don't think sneaking into the boys' camp will impress anyone."

"Maybe you're right. It's got to be something bigger," said a wide-eyed Jessica.

"Bigger!" Elizabeth groaned, hoping that her sister would forget the whole thing. Before she could argue any further, Mrs. Wakefield stuck her head out the kitchen door. "Elizabeth, there's a phone call for you. Don't talk long," she said as she handed her the phone. "We're just about to eat."

At the first sound of Grace Oliver's voice, Elizabeth knew she couldn't hurry the conversation.

"Grace, what is it?" Elizabeth asked with concern.

"I'm definitely not going to camp," Grace said, a note of finality in her voice. "There was no way I could ask my parents without starting another huge fight."

Elizabeth listened as Grace recalled her miserable afternoon. There was a lot of disappointment and hurt in Grace's voice.

When she hung up, Elizabeth stood by the phone for a few minutes. She felt very bad. Camp wouldn't be as much fun without Grace there.

Two

◇

Elizabeth shaded her eyes as she looked around the busy bus terminal. "Do you see Grace anywhere?" she asked Jessica.

"Grace? You told me she wasn't coming."

"She isn't, but the bus to her godmother's house leaves about now. I thought we might run into each other."

Jessica shrugged and sat down on her duffel bag. "This place is packed with people. It's hard enough just keeping track of Mom."

"I guess you're right." Elizabeth sighed.

Just then Mrs. Wakefield hurried over to her daughters. "I checked the schedule and your bus is ready to board in lane four. Are you two all set?"

"We sure are," Jessica said, getting up briskly.

"I wish Daddy and Steven could have come to see us off," Elizabeth commented as they walked to their bus.

"They had to leave early to get good seats for the baseball game in Los Angeles, but Daddy told me to give each of you a kiss for him."

"I bet Steven didn't say that," Jessica said impishly.

"No," her mother agreed, laughing. "He's going to miss you though, I'm sure."

"He'll miss having us to tease," Elizabeth said.

"Oh, no, he won't mind," Jessica retorted. "He'll have three times as much food to eat."

"Well, *I'm* going to miss you both," Mrs. Wakefield said firmly as they stopped in front of the bus that had Camp Loconda posted across the front. She gave them each a hug and a kiss. "Have a terrific time. And don't forget to write."

"We won't," they chorused.

Waving to their mother, the twins climbed happily aboard the bus. It was already filled with other girls from Sweet Valley, and Elizabeth and Jessica had to stop every few rows to say hello to their friends.

"Elizabeth, Jessica, over here," Amy Sutton

called from the back of the bus. "We're saving seats for you."

The twins sat in front of Amy and Ellen Riteman and soon the foursome were giggling about all the fun that was awaiting them at camp. When the bus roared off, someone struck up the song, "One Hundred Bottles of Beer on the Wall." Everyone joined in and when the tune was finished, they followed it up with "The Ants Go Marching One by One." Even the bus driver sang along loudly. The singing made the time fly and soon the bus had left the freeway and was traveling along the narrow country road that led to Camp Loconda.

"Oh, look," Elizabeth squealed as she caught sight of a shimmering body of water. "There's the lake."

"And there are the camp buildings," Jessica said, leaning over her sister to look out the window.

Nestled among the pine trees were a number of picturesque log houses which surrounded a larger building that housed the camp offices and infirmary. As the bus pulled into the driveway, Jessica cried, "Look, horses!"

Several of the girls turned to see a large stable

and riding ring off in the distance behind the administration building. Several horses were standing in the adjoining enclosed pasture.

"I want the chestnut one," Amy said, pointing to a large horse whose tail flicked back and forth.

Elizabeth pressed her nose to the glass. "Oh, but see that one with the spots. He looks like an Indian pony."

As soon as the bus came to a stop, everyone rushed off. There was mass confusion as campers grabbed for their duffel bags and suitcases from the bus's large hold. Counselors, blowing whistles and looking harried, tried to check names off on their clipboards as they directed the girls to their bunks.

An unsmiling teenager with short black hair tapped Jessica on the shoulder. "What's your bunk number?"

"Seven," Jessica answered.

"All right, it's over there, second building from the right," she said curtly.

"She sure wasn't very nice," Elizabeth whispered as she followed Jessica toward the bunk. "I hope she isn't our counselor."

Jessica frowned. "Me, too."

Bunk Seven was already alive with action by the time the twins dragged their bags inside. Kerry Glenn, who had driven up with her parents from Sweet Valley, was unpacking while Kimberly Haver, one of Jessica's Unicorn friends, was changing into a fresh T-shirt. When they caught sight of the twins, both girls greeted them enthusiastically.

A girl they didn't know came out of the bathroom, brushing her hair. "Hi," she said, "I'm Nancy McCall."

Elizabeth smiled, and introduced herself and Jessica. Then Amy and Ellen straggled in with their bags and there were more hellos.

"So this is Bunk Seven," Jessica said, looking around. It was simple but nice: A game table was set up in the front half of the room and four sets of bunk beds stood in the back half. Alongside each set of bunk beds were two small chests of drawers and a small hanging bar for jackets and bathrobes. A single cot for the bunk counselor was positioned by itself in a corner near the doorway. Beyond that was a large bathroom which all the girls were to share.

"This place definitely needs some decoration," Ellen said, eyeing the cabin's bare wood walls.

Kimberly went to her suitcase and pulled out a neatly rolled poster. "What about this?" she asked, unfurling a full-color picture of Kent Kellerman, the sixteen-year-old soap opera star of *All the World*. Squeals of approval erupted.

"Put it up," Nancy implored. "Right on the back of the door, so we can all see Kent before going to sleep."

Kimberly laughed. She took out a roll of tape and was about to hang the poster, when the door flew open and the same counselor who had met the twins coming off the bus stood in the doorway. In her arms were stacks of linens and thin cotton blankets. "The top bunk beds are made already, but you guys need to make the bottom ones. And while you're at it, do the counselor's bed, too." With that brisk order, she put the sheets down on the cot and hurried off.

"Who's she?" Jessica demanded.

Kerry flung her black braid over her shoulder. "One of the counselors, I guess. I got here early, and she's been in a couple of times giving orders."

"Her name is Tina," Kimberly volunteered. "At least, that's what I heard people calling her."

"Do you think she's our bunk counselor?" Elizabeth wanted to know.

"I hope not," Nancy said, making a face.

Amy went over and picked up one of the sheets Tina had dumped on the cot. "Boy, would that be bad luck."

"How in the world can we have any fun with her around?" Ellen asked glumly.

Jessica got an impish grin on her face. "Oh, I don't know. Maybe we'd be able to."

"What do you mean?" Kerry asked, her eyes shining.

Jessica picked up a sheet. "My brother Steven showed me how to short sheet a bed."

"You mean, fold the top sheet over so the person can't get in?" Nancy asked.

Jessica nodded. "Tina *did* ask us to make her bed."

With a whoop of laughter, Kimberly, Kerry, Nancy, and Ellen gathered around Jessica as she unfolded the sheets over the mattress, making sure to tuck them under tightly.

"Tina is going to have a surprise tonight," Kimberly giggled.

"I can hardly wait," Ellen said, fluffing the pillow so the bed looked nice and inviting.

"Maybe next time Tina will be a little more polite," Jessica added, smoothing out the blanket one last time.

Elizabeth didn't mind a practical joke, but hoped Jessica wouldn't get into trouble on her first day at camp. "Jess, do you think that's a good. . . ?" Before she could continue, a pretty blond girl of about seventeen came into the room.

"Hi, everyone. I know things are a little confused around here, but that's typical first day stuff. Everything will settle down and then we can start having fun. Seven's going to be the best bunk at Camp Loconda!"

The girls looked up in surprise. "Who are you?" Jessica asked.

The older girl laughed. "You're right, introductions are in order. I'm Jamie, your counselor."

Uh-oh, Jessica thought. Jamie, not Tina, was going to be their counselor and she seemed really nice. She glanced over at the bed, wondering if she should fix it, or try to explain, but before she could, Jamie started asking them their names.

After the girls introduced themselves, Jamie said, "It's time for the camp tour, and then Mrs. Edwards, the camp director, will give us our orientation. So just stay together and I'll show you around."

As they filed out, Jessica asked, "Who was that other girl, Tina?"

"Oh, Tina's Mrs. Edward's assistant. She works in the office." Jamie winked. "Don't worry, you won't be seeing much of her."

For the next hour, Jamie showed Bunk Seven all that Camp Loconda had to offer. "We use the buddy system for swimming in the lake," she said as they walked along the sandy shore. "Two girls together at all times. We'll be giving swimming tests, so we know how far out you can go, and if you can't swim, we'll teach you."

The water looked so inviting that Elizabeth wished she could put on her suit and jump right in. Her thoughts were interrupted by Jamie talking about the canoes.

"We keep them all over here and they can't be taken out without permission. Each bunk will go on a canoe trip across the lake for an overnight."

"Near the boys' camp?" Jessica asked eagerly.

"It's not far, but Camp Running Bear is off limits to us. There's an old Indian site nearby where we'll be staying."

"What's that?" Amy asked, pointing to a hill close by. It wasn't a very big hill, but it was still significantly higher than the flat land on which the camp was built. A small shack, barely visible from this distance, sat in the center.

Jamie stopped and the girls gathered around her. "That's Crying Moon Mountain."

"Mountain?" Ellen hooted.

"Well, it may not be terribly big, but it has an interesting story. A ghost story," Jamie said mysteriously. "You'll hear it at tonight's campfire."

Elizabeth felt a shiver go down her back. *Crying Moon. What could that mean?* she wondered.

The next stop was the stables, where the girls had a chance to pet the horses. Riding lessons were starting tomorrow. Jamie then showed the campers the arts-and-crafts building where drawings, paintings, and clay sculptures from years past were neatly displayed. Right next door was the recreational building, and behind that stood the dining room where the girls would have their cafeteria-style meals.

"What about sports?" Jessica wanted to know as they walked along. She was very athletic and was one of the stars of Sweet Valley Middle School's basketball team.

"Oh, there are plenty of sports," Jamie responded. "Baseball, archery, volleyball, gymnastics, you name it."

"Wow," Elizabeth whispered to Amy, "the only problem with this camp will be trying to fit everything in."

After the tour, all the campers gathered behind the administration building where Mrs. Edwards welcomed them and introduced all the counselors. Briefly, she went over the camp rules and suggested ways to make the most of their two-week stay.

"Each day your bunk will have different activities," she told them. "At night there will be campfires, and each bunk will be responsible for putting on a skit. There will be all kinds of contests, too, as well as horseback riding, arts and crafts, swimming, and so much more."

"Prizes?" someone asked.

"Oh, definitely," Mrs. Edwards replied. "Trophies will be awarded for the top campers in each event."

Trophies, Jessica thought dreamily. She could already see several of them lined up on her bookshelf at home. Then she had a thought. "Mrs. Edwards," she called out. "Could we do something with the boys at Camp Running Bear?"

Mrs. Edwards looked startled. "We never have."

"But maybe we could have a dance," Jessica persisted.

"I'll have to think about it," Mrs. Edwards said. She called on another camper whose hand was raised.

Good, Jessica thought. *And I'll think about it, too.*

After lunch, the afternoon went by in a flash. The girls wrote postcards home during rest period and then played a long game of volleyball. Before supper they all went into the lake for the refreshing swim Elizabeth had been hoping for.

"What are you going to do about Jamie's bed?" Elizabeth asked Jessica as the two splashed each other.

"What can I do? I'd fix it, but she hasn't let us out of her sight." Jessica dived under the water and came up laughing. Her little prank was obviously not worrying her too much.

After a "Welcome to Camp" dinner of fried chicken, corn on the cob, and cherry pie, everyone headed outdoors for the first evening campfire. They strolled to a wooded area near the stables to pick up sticks for roasting marshmallows before heading to a nearby clearing.

"Gee, it's pretty out here," Elizabeth said as

she settled herself between Jessica and Amy.

Jessica looked up at the tall pine trees swaying in the wind, and the stars twinkling down at them from the dusky sky. "Sure is."

"But it's a little creepy, too," Amy added. "I'm glad there're so many of us out here."

"Oh, come on, scaredy-cat," Jessica scoffed. "Even if we were by ourselves, it's just the great outdoors. What's to be frightened of?"

"Nothing, I think," said Amy as she settled in for an evening of spooky stories.

Tina started off. "A couple was driving through the country when their convertible broke down in the woods. As night fell, they pulled the roof shut over them. Soon after, they heard a strange scratching sound on top of the car. Frightened, the couple huddled together. They could see nothing in the darkness and tried to reassure each other that a tree branch was probably brushing against the canvas rooftop. But the scratching continued, and soon a small hole appeared above their heads. They realized that whatever was above the car was wearing out the canvas. In a panic, the couple tried to open the doors to get out, but the doors wouldn't unlock. The woman shrieked as the hole became larger and they saw a body hanging from a tree limb, the soles of its feet scraping through the roof. It was too late. The rope broke and with a crash, the body tore through the rooftop, feetfirst."

All the girls screamed and shrieked. Hearing the story with only the crackling campfire to give them light had made the whole thing seem frighteningly real.

Next, it was Jamie's turn. "Once upon a time, a handsome man married a beautiful woman who always wore a black velvet ribbon around her neck. The man thought the ribbon was a pretty decoration, but when the woman did not ever take it off, even at night, he became curious. He asked her repeatedly why she never took off the velvet ribbon, and she would say, 'Because I mustn't.' Thinking that a priceless gift would change her mind, he bought her a diamond and ruby choker. But she still refused to take off the ribbon. As they lay in bed that night, the man looked at his sleeping wife. Her beauty brought a smile to his face, but then his gaze fell upon her neck. Slowly, he brought his hand up and untied the black velvet ribbon. His eyes widened and he screamed as his wife's head broke away from her neck and rolled to the floor."

"Oh, my gosh!" exclaimed several girls.

"Still feeling brave?" Amy whispered to Jessica.

"Of course I am," Jessica said, sticking out her chin. But she wasn't so sure.

"I'll tell the last story," Mrs. Edwards said. "It's a local legend many townspeople believe. It has to do with that hill." She pointed to Crying Moon Mountain. "At one time, this was all Indian country and two enemy tribes lived here. One day, an Indian maiden named Crying Moon was picking flowers on top of the hill when she was surprised by Running Bear, a young brave from the other tribe. At first Crying Moon was frightened, but Running Bear spoke to her gently and helped to gather flowers for her bouquet. Soon they fell in love and kept coming back to the hill to meet. More than anything, they wanted to be together."

The girls leaned forward, half-eaten marshmallows forgotten on their sticks.

"This is so romantic," Elizabeth whispered, and Jessica nodded.

"Then, one summer evening, Crying Moon went to the hill but Running Bear never came. Crying Moon waited and waited, then went back to her camp. There she heard some terrible news.

A brave from the other tribe had been captured. 'What does he look like?' she asked anxiously. An old woman described Running Bear. He had been on his way up the hill to meet Crying Moon when he had been spotted by her tribe, captured, and killed."

"Oh, no," Jessica gasped.

"Poor Crying Moon went mad with grief. She thought Running Bear was still alive, and each day she would climb up the hill and search frantically for him. During a violent rainstorm, lightning struck her and she collapsed on the hill. Those who ran after her claimed that before dying she called out for Running Bear."

Elizabeth felt tears welling up in her eyes, and several girls around the circle were sniffling.

"Even today," Mrs. Edwards continued, "people often think they can see Crying Moon on the hill, a torch in her hand, looking for Running Bear. When the wind whistles, they say you can hear her calling his name."

A long silence followed the end of the story. Mrs. Edwards broke the mood by starting the camp song, "Hail, Hail, Camp Loconda."

On the way back to the bunk, Elizabeth, Amy, and Jessica discussed the tale. "Do you think it really could have happened?" Elizabeth wondered.

"It was so long ago," Amy said doubtfully.

"But it was so romantic. That's why people still remember it," Jessica insisted.

The girls stopped and looked over in the direction of the hill. "And they still think they see Crying Moon," Amy said with a sigh.

"Oh, I don't believe that part of it. There are no such things as ghosts," Elizabeth said.

Jessica shrugged. "Maybe, maybe not."

While Elizabeth and Amy walked on, Jessica stood and stared toward the hill. It was dark, but the moon shining down on it outlined its craggy face. Jessica was about to turn away when a flickering light coming from the direction of the hill caught her eye.

Jessica stood still. A light? How was that possible? Unless the legend of Crying Moon was true! Jessica strained to see in the darkness. The light was only a tiny beam, but it was there.

"Elizabeth, Amy, come back here!" Jessica called in an excited voice. "Look over there," she said, pointing in the direction of the hill. "There's a light coming from the hill. Maybe it's Crying Moon!"

"Where?" Elizabeth said, hurrying over and peering into the darkness.

Amy looked, too. "I don't see a thing."

Jessica was ready to argue, but now, looking closely, she couldn't see anything either. "Well, it was there," she said defensively.

"Oh, stop teasing, Jess."

"No, really, I'm sure I saw it, Liz," Jessica insisted. "It must have been the ghost of Crying Moon."

"But, Jessica, there are no such things as ghosts," Amy said sensibly. "I agree with Elizabeth."

"You're sure of that?"

"Of course," Elizabeth replied.

"Then I dare you to go to the top of the hill tomorrow night and check it out for yourselves."

"We can't do that," Elizabeth said.

"Because you're afraid."

"Don't be silly. It's just that we wouldn't be allowed."

"It'll be the middle of the night," Jessica argued. "No one will even know you're gone. Unless, of course, you're just too afraid you'll see the ghost of Crying Moon."

"That's ridiculous," Elizabeth said. She

looked up at the hill. Climbing to the top didn't seem all that difficult. "All right, I'll take you up on your dare. I'm not afraid of something that doesn't exist."

"I'm not, either," Amy added.

"Fine. Then tomorrow night you'll find out for sure."

"No problem," Elizabeth said, sounding braver than she actually felt. It was one thing to climb the hill, but what would she and Amy find?

Yawning, the girls barely talked as they entered their bunk, washed up, and brushed their teeth. It had been such a full day that all the campers were ready to turn in.

"Do you want the top bunk or the bottom?" Elizabeth asked Jessica as she pulled on her pajama top.

"Oh, bottom, I guess." Then, Jessica clapped her hand over her mouth. "I forgot about Jamie's bed!"

"You'd better tell her," Elizabeth said.

Jessica nodded, but before she could tell Jamie what she had done, a shriek came from the cot in the corner of the room.

"Hey, what's this?"

Someone flicked on the light and all the girls

laughed to see Jamie tangled up in the sheets. Jessica was relieved to see that Jamie was giggling, too.

"Usually the campers wait until later to try something like this," she said good-naturedly.

Jessica and Elizabeth helped Jamie remake her bed. Then the lights were turned off again, and after a few whispers, most of the girls fell asleep.

Elizabeth listened to the steady breathing coming from Amy, who had the top bunk across from her. Jessica was sound asleep, too. But no matter how she tossed and turned, Elizabeth couldn't make herself comfortable. Her thoughts were on the visit to Crying Moon Mountain she had promised to make the following night. *You're being silly*, she told herself. She punched her pillow and settled down once more. *After all, there couldn't be ghosts up on that hill, could there?*

Three

◇

"A treasure hunt!" Jessica exclaimed. "That sounds like fun."

The twins' second day at Camp Loconda was off to a busy start. The morning had begun with swimming tests, which both Elizabeth and Jessica had passed with flying colors. They would be allowed to swim as far as the float in the middle of the lake. Now Jamie was telling Bunk Seven about the treasure hunt. The girls huddled around her in the middle of the room, their eyes glowing with excitement.

Jamie held up a piece of paper. "There are ten clues in all. I start you out with the first clue. If you interpret it correctly, it will lead you to the next clue. Keep going, and you'll find the treasure. Besides being fun, this is a good way to familiarize yourselves with the campgrounds."

"What about the other bunks?" Jessica asked.

"They each have the same clues, but every group will start with a different one, so you all begin in different places. But all clues lead to the treasure."

Elizabeth raised her hand. "What is the treasure?"

Jamie's eyes twinkled. "You'll find out. If you get to the treasure first, of course."

There was excited chatter among the campers. "Let's get started," Ellen said. But before Jamie could hand them their first clue, one of the counselors came up to their group with a sullen-looking girl whose brown hair hung limply around her face.

"We have too many teams," the counselor told Jamie, "so we're dividing the girls in Bunk Three up among the other groups. Barbara Fields will be joining yours," she said, leaving Barbara standing in the middle of the circle as she hurried away.

"Welcome, Barbara," Jamie said with a smile, but Barbara's scowl only deepened.

"Well," Jamie said, taken aback. "I guess you can introduce yourselves as the treasure hunt goes on." She looked around. "We'd better get started; some of the other teams already have their clues. Jessica, why don't you be the team captain?" Jamie handed her the folded piece of paper that held the first clue.

"Open it," Ellen demanded.

"I am," Jessica said, smoothing the paper flat. Then she read aloud the rhyme that was printed on the paper.

> "Girls aren't the only ones
> Who have to brush their hair
> Go to a certain place—
> Ponytails are there."

The girls looked at each other blankly.

"Hair? What about a beauty shop?" Nancy asked.

"There's no beauty shop at camp," Ellen scoffed.

"Wait! Ponytails!" Elizabeth said. "It must mean the stable."

With a whoop, the girls ran off in the direction of the stables. Only Barbara lagged behind, looking as if she didn't care if the next clue were found or not.

Once inside the stable, Kerry held up her hands and asked, "Now where?"

"This place is huge," Nancy agreed.

"Well, let's spread out," Jessica ordered. "Everyone take a section of the building and start looking."

The girls were looking feverishly through the stalls and in every corner of the stable when Barbara sauntered into the barn. "Haven't you found that clue yet?" she asked.

Jessica looked up from the wool blanket she was examining, "No," she said curtly.

Elizabeth tried to be a little friendlier. "Do you have any ideas?"

"Sure," Barbara answered, "didn't the clue say something about brushing hair?"

Jessica pulled the clue out of her pocket, and the others stopped to listen. "Yes, 'Girls aren't the only ones who have to brush their hair,'" she read.

Barbara shrugged as if the answer were simple. "Then the next clue is probably by the brushes and combs."

"Let's check," Elizabeth said.

There was a huge cardboard box with steel

combs and brushes sitting on the windowsill. The girls rushed over, and sure enough, tucked away in the corner of the box was a piece of white paper, folded just as their original clue was.

"This is it," Jessica said, as she plucked it from its hiding place. She hesitated, then she handed it to Barbara. "I guess you should read it."

Barbara made a face, but she took the paper anyway.

> "People have houses.
> These do, too.
> It's near the water
> In plain view."
> (PUT THIS CLUE BACK
> FOR THE NEXT SEEKERS.)

This clue was easy to figure out. Almost immediately Amy, Elizabeth, and several of the other girls shouted, "The boathouse!"

On their way down to the lake, the girls passed several other groups of campers heading this way and that, wherever their clues were leading them. At the boathouse, which was filled with canoes and rowboats, the girls of Bunk Seven scattered, looking for their tiny piece of white paper.

This time it took even longer, and Jessica began to worry that the other teams were getting ahead of them.

"You know, there's a faster way to be doing this," Barbara said, hands on hips.

The girls stopped and looked at her. "What do you mean?" Jessica demanded.

"Why should we break our necks looking for the clues? We could just send someone outside to listen to the other groups and see what they're finding. Things are so confused, no one would notice an extra girl running around."

"Barbara, that's cheating," a shocked Elizabeth said.

"I think it's just being smart." She shrugged.

"I don't want to do anything like that," Jessica replied in a stiff tone. "If we look a little harder, we'll find it."

"It doesn't matter to me," Barbara said. She started looking around again, halfheartedly.

Amy finally found the clue hidden in one of the boats, but the girls of Bunk Seven had lost valuable time. The next clue led them to the dining room, and the one after that to the arts-and-crafts building. Before they could look for any more clues, though, they heard screaming. "We found it, we found it!" Campers from all over started running to the little grove of trees near the campfire site where Bunk One had dug up an old wooden treasure chest.

"Oh, great! Paperback books," one of the winners cried as she opened the chest.

Someone held up a book and Elizabeth could see it was a copy of the brand-new Amanda Howard mystery. Amanda Howard was her favorite writer.

"Are you disappointed?" Amy asked, coming up behind her. Amanda Howard was one of her favorites, too.

Elizabeth nodded. "Maybe they'll pass the books around when they're done reading them."

"At least we didn't cheat to get the treasure," Amy said.

Elizabeth stared at Barbara, who was standing by herself outside the circle. "I wonder what her problem is."

"I don't know," Amy said. "But she definitely has one."

That afternoon, during rest period, the topic of Barbara came up again.

"She's weird," Nancy remarked.

"Did you notice she wasn't in the dining

room at lunch?" Jessica asked. "I asked one of her bunkmates where she was, and the girl said Barbara told her counselor she didn't feel like eating and then took off."

"Oh, who cares?" Ellen said, flipping through a fashion magazine. "Let her be by herself if she wants."

"She sure wasn't much fun," Kerry agreed.

"If she doesn't shape up, she might not get invited to the dance," Jessica said casually.

Kimberly sat straight up in her bed. "Dance? What dance?"

"I thought Mrs. Edwards said we didn't have any activities planned with the boys from Camp Running Bear," Ellen said.

Jessica smiled. "We don't yet."

Elizabeth knew that look in her twin's eye all too well. "What do you have planned, Jessica?"

Jessica leaned forward, her eyes shining. "I think Camp Loconda should listen to the campers' opinions about activities. Don't you?"

"Of course," Ellen said and the others nodded.

"So, wouldn't a dance be fun?"

"It sure would," Kerry said.

"It would be fabulous," Kimberly agreed.

Jessica pulled a piece of paper from under her pillow. "I've been working on this. It's a petition. It says, 'We the Undersigned want to have a dance with the boys from Camp Running Bear.'"

"Where do I sign?" Nancy cried.

Jessica passed the petition around and everyone signed it. Elizabeth didn't care much about a dance one way or the other, but she wanted to support her sister. She took a pen and put her name on the bottom of the list.

"I'll pass it around tonight at supper," Jessica said, scanning the names with satisfaction. "We'll have so many signatures that Mrs. Edwards will just have to let us have a dance."

"We're having a barbecue tonight for supper," Elizabeth reminded her twin.

"That's all right," Jessica said. "I'll bring a flashlight."

Ellen made a face. "I hope there're not going to be any more ghost stories. I was really scared last night."

"Do you think that story they told about Crying Moon could be true?" Nancy asked thoughtfully.

"Well, I guess we're going to find out for sure tonight," Jessica told the group.

They looked at each other. "What do you mean?" Kimberly wanted to know.

In hushed tones, Jessica told the girls about the flickering light she had seen the night before. "Elizabeth and Amy said there aren't any such things as ghosts, so they're going to go up there tonight to check it out for themselves."

"No!" Kerry said. "Really?"

Elizabeth got a sinking feeling in the pit of her stomach. With all the day's exciting activities, she had pushed Jessica's dare out of her mind. But now, with her bunkmates staring at her, she didn't see how she could get out of it. "I guess so," she said slowly.

"You too, Amy?" the girls asked.

Amy nodded. "There aren't any ghosts. There's nothing to be scared of." Her voice sounded brave, but she was nervously folding and unfolding her hands.

The barbecue was not followed by more spooky stories. Instead, Bunk Two presented a skit about a princess who falls in love with a rock star. During the performance, Elizabeth tried to think of a way to get out of her dare. She kept hoping that Amy would say she didn't want to go through with it.

But whenever Elizabeth caught her friend's eye, Amy smiled and gave her the thumbs-up sign as if she didn't have a care in the world.

Walking back to the bunk after the campfire, Jessica chattered about all the signatures she had gotten on her petition. "I got everyone in Bunk Five and Six to sign," she said with satisfaction. "And most of the girls in Bunk One."

"But Jessica, what about the boys?" Nancy asked.

"The boys?"

"How do we know they want to have a dance with us?"

"Oh, I'm sure they do," Jessica answered confidently.

"Could you prove that to Mrs. Edwards?" Nancy asked.

Jessica stopped and faced her. "You mean you think I should get their signatures on the petition, too?"

"Well, it makes sense, doesn't it?" Nancy continued. "Think how embarrassing it will be if we hand in our petition and the boys say they don't want a dance."

"I guess you're right."

"So far we haven't seen the boys at all. It

won't be easy to get their signatures," Ellen warned.

"No, but it might be fun to try," Jessica said, her eyes sparkling at the idea. "I'd have to go over to Camp Running Bear and ask the boys to sign."

"Wow, Jessica's not afraid of anything, is she?" Amy whispered in Elizabeth's ear.

Elizabeth shook her head. "No, my twin is pretty fearless." She turned to Amy. "What about you? How do you feel about climbing up to Crying Moon Mountain tonight?"

"How do you feel about it?"

"I don't want to do it," Elizabeth said in a soft voice.

"You don't? I don't either."

"Why didn't you say so earlier?" Elizabeth asked with surprise. "I thought it didn't bother you."

"I thought I'd be letting you down. Besides, I was afraid the others would laugh if we chickened out. Jessica did get all the girls excited about it."

"I know what you mean," Elizabeth said with a sigh. "Jessica's good at stirring things up. We'll just have to be brave."

All of Bunk Seven was overflowing with anticipation at the upcoming excursion, but the girls tried to act normal as they got ready for bed. It wasn't until the lights were off and Jamie was fast asleep that Jessica sat up in bed and leaned over to whisper to her sister. "It's time," she announced.

Slowly, Elizabeth got out of bed and put on the clothes she had folded and placed under her pillow. Amy got up and got dressed, too.

Jessica handed Elizabeth the flashlight she had used at the campfire. "Don't forget this, Liz," she whispered.

As they headed for the door, Ellen called in a soft voice, "Good luck."

"We'll be waiting for a report," Nancy reminded them.

Outside, the air was crisp and sweet. Elizabeth looked up at Crying Moon Mountain. The shack was easy to see against the full moon and starry sky.

"At least there're no lights on tonight," Elizabeth said with relief.

"So you believe Jessica?" Amy asked. "You think she really did see a light in the cabin?"

"I don't know," Elizabeth said grimly, "but I guess we're going to find out."

Slowly, the girls made their way toward the hill, walking carefully through the underbrush.

The camp was still and quiet and the only noise, apart from the crickets chirping, was the sound of twigs breaking softly under their feet.

"You know, we could just tell them we went up there," Amy suggested. "No one would ever know the difference."

"We would know," Elizabeth answered. "We said we would do it, and we have to go through with it."

"I guess you're right," Amy said, sounding unenthusiastic.

The girls passed the stables and then headed toward the path that led up the hill.

"It sure is a long way," Amy said, pointing the flashlight in the direction of the shack.

"Then we'd better hurry it up," Elizabeth said in a take-charge tone.

She had only taken a few steps when she felt something grab her arm. A small scream escaped Elizabeth's throat.

"Quiet, Lizzie. It's only me."

"Jessica!" Elizabeth cried, her terror mixed with relief. "You scared me to death. What are you doing here?"

"It didn't seem right," Jessica said uncomfortably. "I mean, I dared you to come out here, but it could be dangerous. The least I could do was come along."

Elizabeth felt her anger melting. She couldn't deny that she was happy to see her sister. "I'm glad you did."

"Me, too," Amy said. "If there are ghosts up there, I want as many people with us as possible."

"Well, let's get going," Jessica said, trying to ignore the butterflies fluttering around in her stomach. It was one thing to dare Elizabeth and Amy to climb the hill at night, but now that she was with them in the darkness, it didn't seem quite so funny.

Even with the flashlight and the moon and stars casting a faint light, it was difficult for the trio to make their way up Crying Moon Mountain. Stones and boulders were everywhere, and the trip seemed to take twice as long as it would have in the daytime.

"What's that noise?" Elizabeth said, stopping in her tracks.

"I didn't hear anything," Jessica replied. But she looked around anyway.

Another distinct scream pierced the air. This time it sounded as though it were closer to them.

"It's an owl, isn't it?" Amy asked in a shaky voice.

"I thought owls made a hooting noise," Elizabeth responded. "Maybe it's a bobcat or something."

Jessica turned and looked back toward the camp. "We've come more than halfway. We might as well just keep going," she prodded.

"Then let's hurry," Elizabeth said.

Running and stumbling, the girls made their way up the hill. Elizabeth stubbed her toe on a large rock, but she picked herself up and kept going. She didn't want to be out any longer than she had to be. She hoped they could take a quick look around the shack and get back to the bunk without Jamie waking up. Elizabeth sighed. She wished she were snuggled up safely in her bunk bed right now.

Finally, the dilapidated shack was only a few yards from them.

"It looks deserted," Amy said, her voice barely audible.

"It sure does," Elizabeth agreed.

Jessica hoped her voice sounded brave. "Good. Then we won't have any problems."

They stood there, not one of them eager to take the first step.

"Let's go," Jessica said at last. "Follow me."

Creeping as silently as the Indians in Crying

Moon's story, the girls moved toward the cabin. When they were close enough, they peered through the window, but they couldn't see a thing.

"Maybe the door is locked," Amy said hopefully.

They crept over to the wooden door, and touched it gently. The door creaked open. Clasping hands, Jessica, Elizabeth, and Amy stepped into the inky blackness.

As their eyes adjusted to the light, the girls could see that they were in a small room that had a rusty sink and an old table surrounded by several broken-down chairs. A large stone fireplace took up most of one wall and a doorway next to it led to another room.

"There's nothing here," Elizabeth said nervously. "Let's go back now."

"Do you think we should see what's in the other room?" Jessica asked.

"No!" Amy and Elizabeth said in unison.

"All right," Jessica agreed. "Let's get out of here."

The girls turned, anxious to make their escape, when suddenly a bright light shone on the front door.

"What's that?" Jessica said, her voice quavering.

Then Elizabeth screamed. Outlined against the yellow glow was a huge, dark shadow blocking their way to safety.

Four

◇

For a few seconds the girls remained frozen to the spot. Then, with screams and shrieks, they flew out the door and began to run down the hill. A voice behind them called out, "Elizabeth, don't go! It's me."

Elizabeth stopped running and turned back towards the shack. There, outlined in the door was a small figure with curly hair. There was no mistaking it. It was Grace Oliver!

"Jess, Amy, come back!" Elizabeth shouted down the hill. "It's Grace."

Hurrying back to the shack, Elizabeth stared at Grace. "What on earth are you doing here? We thought you were the Ghost of Crying Moon Mountain."

Before Grace could say a word, Jessica and Amy appeared, huffing and puffing. Jessica leaned against a tree, trying to catch her breath. "Where . . . where did you come from?"

"You scared us half to death," Amy said accusingly.

"I'm sorry," Grace said. "You'd better come in and I'll explain it all to you."

Inside the shack, the girls could see that the glowing bright light which had frightened them so badly came from a kerosene lamp that was sitting in the corner of the room.

"Wow," Elizabeth said, taking a seat on one of the old chairs. "You should have seen your shadow. It was big enough to be a monster."

Grace gave a shaky laugh. "How do you think I felt when I heard whispering in here? I thought for sure it was robbers coming back to their hiding place."

Jessica stood with her arms folded. "Grace, tell us. What are you doing here? I thought Elizabeth said you had to go to your godmother's house."

"I did," Grace admitted. "At least I was supposed to. But I changed my mind."

Elizabeth watched as Grace nervously twisted a curl around her finger. "I think you'd better tell us the whole story, starting at the very beginning," she said soothingly.

Grace sat down next to Elizabeth. "Remember I told you that the bus to my godmother's was leaving about the same time as the buses for Camp Loconda?"

Elizabeth nodded. "Sure. I even looked around for you at the bus station."

"My mother and I arrived just as you and Jessica were getting on the bus. I could see everybody getting on board, laughing and looking like they were going to have a great time. My mother was in a hurry, so she just put me on my bus. She didn't have time to wait and see me off." Grace stared into the lamplight, remembering. "I was looking out the window, seeing the camp buses filling up, and I decided I wanted to go, too. It wasn't fair that I had to go to my godmother's while the rest of you were coming up here for two weeks of fun," she said with anger in her voice.

"Then what happened?" Jessica asked, her eyes wide.

"Luckily, my bus was right near a bank of phones. I called my godmother and left a message on her answering machine saying my mother and I had decided to go on a cruise. That way she wouldn't try to get in touch with Mom," Grace said with satisfaction.

"What about your father?" Elizabeth wanted to know.

"He's on a fishing trip. I don't think there are too many phones around there."

"So then you snuck onto one of the camp buses?" Amy guessed.

Grace nodded. "That's right. I watched to see which buses didn't have any kids from Sweet Valley and I got on one of those."

"Didn't anyone notice you?"

"Nope. Everything was sort of confused, so I took a seat at the back and stayed there."

"What happened when we arrived at camp?" Elizabeth asked.

"That was a problem," Grace said with a sigh. "The counselors were checking off names and everything. I didn't know what to do. Then I saw this cabin on the hill and I came up here. It had running water, and the lamp, and some canned food." Grace made a face. "I've been eating cold spaghetti and sardines."

"Gross," Jessica said.

"But what are you going to do?" Elizabeth said. "How long can you stay up here?"

Grace shook her head. "To tell you the truth, I was thinking about turning myself in and going to my godmother's house. I'm not really having any fun up here by myself."

"Gee, that would be a shame after you've gone through so much trouble to get here," Jessica said.

"I don't think Grace has much of a choice," Elizabeth cut in.

"I wouldn't say that."

"What do you mean, Jessica?" a puzzled Grace asked.

Jessica leaned toward them. "Well, think about it. Now that Grace is here, why shouldn't she have some fun at camp? No one will be looking for her. Her godmother thinks she's on a cruise, and her parents think she's with her godmother. And she *is* safe here at camp."

"That's true," Elizabeth said slowly.

"There are so many girls at camp," Jessica continued in an excited voice. "Who would notice one extra?"

"Where would Grace sleep?" Amy interjected.

Jessica thought about that for a moment. "It's too bad she can't stay in Bunk Seven. We do have an empty bed, but I guess she'll have to sleep up here. There's no way we could hide her from Jamie at night."

"I wouldn't mind sleeping here," Grace said eagerly. "Not if I could hang around with you guys all day."

Elizabeth had a few misgivings about the plan. Could Grace sneak into the dining room? What if one of the counselors realized she didn't belong? But Grace looked so happy, she couldn't bear to bring these problems up. "I suppose it would work."

"Sure it would," Jessica said, her eyes shining.

"You'll love camp," Amy told Grace. "There're so many fantastic things to do."

"I know. I've been watching you all day, wishing I could be down there with you."

Hearing Grace's longing, Elizabeth reached over and patted her hand. "Well, now you're going to be."

Amy glanced at her watch. "Oh, gosh! We'd better get back to the bunk. The other girls might think we're lost."

"Or grabbed by the ghost of Crying Moon." Jessica grinned.

"Who is that?" asked a confused Grace.

"We'll tell you all about it tomorrow," Elizabeth promised, "but Amy's right. We've got to get back right now."

"Just come down around breakfast time," Jessica said. "We'll meet you in front of the dining room. No one takes attendance, and there's always a bunch of girls going inside between eight and nine."

Going down the hill was a lot easier than getting up had been. Now that the girls were familiar with the path, they quickly made their way back to camp.

When they neared the silent bunks, Jessica put her finger to her lips. On tiptoe, the trio passed the administration building where Mrs. Edwards slept. With sighs of relief, they finally made it to the safety of Bunk Seven.

Opening the door slowly so it wouldn't creak, the three slipped inside. Several of the girls sat up in bed, and Ellen whispered angrily, "Where were you? I was just about to wake Jamie and tell her you were missing."

Jessica glanced over in Jamie's direction, glad to see that she was still sleeping, her blanket pulled up to her chin. "Sorry," she said. "You won't believe what happened."

"Did you see any ghosts?" Kerry asked anxiously.

"No, but we did find something." Jessica looked at Jamie, who was now moving restlessly in her bed.

"What?" Ellen demanded.

"Not now. We'll tell you all about it in the morning."

The girls of Bunk Seven got up early the next morning and gathered in the bathroom where they could have some privacy. Quickly, Jessica told them about finding Grace and explained their friend's predicament. The girls reacted with surprise, then delight. Grace was well-liked by those who knew her from Sweet Valley. All the girls agreed it would be a lot of fun to make her a part of Camp Loconda.

As usual there was much commotion in the dining room as the girls lined up for breakfast. No one noticed that today there was one extra redhaired camper waiting for her bacon and eggs.

When Bunk Seven sat down to eat, everyone excitedly greeted Grace. All of the girls told her how much fun she was going to have at camp.

"What activity do we have after breakfast?" Grace asked happily.

"Swimming," Elizabeth answered, "but there might be a problem with that."

"How come?"

"We have to swim with a buddy and you make an extra person."

The girls looked at each other. Then Ellen spoke up. "I don't mind missing swimming. Grace can wear my suit and my bathing cap. Everyone will think she's me."

"What a good idea," Jessica said with admiration. "Let's hurry up with breakfast and get Grace into your swimsuit."

A half hour later, Bunk Seven headed down to the lake. "So far so good," Elizabeth whispered to Grace.

Jamie and Rose, the swimming instructor, were down at the lake with the girls, but they didn't notice anything unusual. When Jamie took her head count, Grace turned her back, and Jamie just checked her off. Once she was in the water, neither Rose nor Jamie paid any further attention.

"Hey, this is easy," Grace laughed as she swam by Jessica.

Jessica gave her the thumbs-up sign.

But changing back to clothes after the swim was a little more complicated. Jamie was now walking in and out of the bunk as the girls showered and changed. There was no way Grace could hide behind Ellen's bathing suit and cap now.

Grace was shivering, hiding in a toilet stall when Jamie once again strolled into the bathroom. "Hurry up, you guys. It's almost time for the baseball game." She sauntered over to the mirror and started brushing her hair.

Elizabeth and Jessica, both dressed, looked at each other in horror. How long was Jamie intending to stay there, fooling with her hair?

"Uh, Jamie," Elizabeth said, coming up behind her. "Did you see those strange tracks outside our cabin?"

Jamie looked at Elizabeth's reflection in the mirror. "What tracks?" she frowned.

"Big tracks," Elizabeth replied, making her eyes wide. "Right near the door."

Jamie frowned. "It could be deer, but maybe I should check it out. Let's go look."

Elizabeth looked at Jessica in relief as she followed Jamie out of the bathroom.

"Quick," Jessica said, knocking at the stall door. "Come out and get dressed, Grace."

"I thought I was never going to get out of there," Grace said, throwing off her towel and putting on the clothes Jessica handed her.

"We really need to be on our toes if we intend to keep you hidden," Jessica said.

Ellen stuck her head into the bathroom. "They're coming back," she warned.

Grace pulled her T-shirt over her head and looked around. "I can go out the window."

Jessica ran over and held up the window while Grace slipped out. "Meet us at the playing field," Jessica whispered. She was back at the sink, washing her hands when Jamie came back in.

"Ready for baseball?" Jamie asked.

"Sure," Jessica replied. "Did you see those tracks?"

Jamie shook her head. "Someone must have scuffed them up. By the time I got out there, they were gone."

"Too bad," Jessica said as she followed Jamie out the door.

After a hard-fought baseball game in which Grace blended in with the rest of the campers, it was time for the Bunk Seven campers to plan their skit for the evening. They went over to the rec building where the costumes were kept, while Grace strolled around the camp.

"Do you want me to stay with you?" Jamie asked.

"Oh, that's all right," Jessica said casually. "We can plan it ourselves. That way it will be a surprise for you, too."

An agreeable Jamie left them to their planning and Elizabeth ran outside to find Grace.

Once everyone was present, Nancy asked, "Do you think Grace should be in our play or would that be pressing our luck?"

"Maybe I shouldn't," Grace said worriedly. "If I got up in front of everyone, I'm sure I'd be noticed."

"Not if you were wearing a mask," Jessica answered with a gleam in her eye.

All the girls started talking at the same time. "A mask!" "What a great idea!"

"We could all wear masks," Amy piped up.

"And I have a great idea for a skit," Elizabeth said. "We could act out the story of Crying Moon and Running Bear."

"Now just who are those two?" Grace wanted to know. "I keep hearing their names."

Quickly, the girls filled Grace in on the story. Then they planned their reenactment. There were enough roles for everyone. As they started looking through the trunks filled with costumes, the girls came up with a few suitable shirts and dresses as well as several hairpieces that they could turn into braided wigs. Then they found some construction paper and markers to make their masks.

When it was time for the campfire, the girls from Bunk Seven were excited and ready to go. If they could pull this off, they were sure no one would ever find out that there was one extra camper in their midst.

As they walked to the campfire, Elizabeth pulled Jessica over to the side. "Jess, I'm worried," she said in a low voice. "We're taking a big chance."

"Come on, Lizzie. Grace will be wearing a black wig with braids and a mask. No one will know who she is."

"But Jamie might count the campers," Elizabeth protested.

"Why would she do that?" Jessica asked practically. "We'll all be running in and out of the woods the whole time. She'll never keep track of us and she won't even try."

"I hope you're right," Elizabeth said nervously.

Jessica patted her on the shoulder. "Don't worry, Liz, this is going to be easy."

And to Elizabeth's amazement, it was. Grace sat at the campfire singing songs and roasting marshmallows with the rest of the Camp Loconda girls, and no one paid the least bit of attention to her. When it was time for the skit, Jessica got up and made a long introduction, giving her bunkmates and Grace time to get into their costumes. All eyes were on Jessica and her dramatic introduction to the tale. Neither the counselors nor Mrs. Edwards watched the girls putting on their outfits and masks behind the tall pine trees.

Elizabeth took the part of Crying Moon, and Nancy, the tallest of the girls, was Running Bear. Grace proudly went on stage as Crying Moon's mother. During the skit, Elizabeth nervously peered into the audience to see if anyone seemed to notice anything strange, but they all were enthralled with the reenactment of the dramatic tale.

As the campfire dimmed, the girls ended the evening as they always did, with the Camp Loconda song. Then everyone drifted back to their bunks. Grace, still wearing her wig, faded into the forest, heading back to the cabin on the hill.

"What a terrific night," Jessica said as she strolled along with Elizabeth, Amy, and Ellen.

"It worked out better than we ever dreamed," Ellen said with satisfaction.

"I'm so glad that Grace is having a good

time," Elizabeth said. "She really deserves it after all the problems she's had at home."

"She told me it was one of the best nights of her life," Amy informed them.

"Well, if we could parade her right in front of the whole camp, I guess we can do just about anything," Jessica said with satisfaction. "Grace can spend as much time as she wants with us and no one will ever know the difference."

One by one, the girls of Bunk Seven filed into their cabin, but Elizabeth lingered outside. The air was so sweet here at camp, with just a hint of a breeze blowing through the pines.

After staring at the stars, Elizabeth turned to go inside when she felt a tap on her shoulder.

"Oh!" she cried, jumping a little. "You startled me."

Barbara looked at her with hard, dark eyes. "I was just wondering, Elizabeth. Who was that new girl in your skit?"

There was a quaver in Elizabeth's voice as she answered, "New girl? What new girl?"

"I thought I saw someone with red hair putting on a mask behind the trees. You didn't have a red-haired girl in your bunk during the treasure hunt."

"It was so dark. You must have made a mistake." Elizabeth hated lying, but she didn't see what choice she had.

"Did I? Well, maybe," Barbara said.

"It was just the regular crew." Elizabeth gave what she hoped was a casual shrug.

"So you're still short a girl in your bunk, then?"

Elizabeth pointed into the window of the brightly lit cabin, where the girls inside were talking and giggling while they got ready for bed. "See? The same kids as yesterday."

Barbara followed Elizabeth's gaze, then she turned away. Without even a goodnight, Barbara headed back to her own bunk.

Elizabeth stood looking after her. *Oh, no,* Elizabeth thought to herself. If there was one person she wished wouldn't discover their secret, it was Barbara. Moody and unfriendly, Barbara Fields made her nervous.

Elizabeth opened the door to the cabin with a heavy heart. She couldn't quite put her finger on the reason, but she had a strong suspicion that Barbara Fields was going to cause Bunk Seven nothing but trouble.

Five

◇

Elizabeth slipped inside the cabin and pulled Jessica off to the side.

"What is it?" Jessica asked irritably. "I was just about to get into bed."

"We have a problem," Elizabeth informed her. Then she quickly recounted her conversation with Barbara.

Jessica frowned, then her face cleared. "I don't think that's any big deal, Lizzie. After all, Barbara really didn't see a thing. All she has are her suspicions."

"That's true."

"And without any proof, she wouldn't dare

try anything," Jessica added, patting her sister on the shoulder.

"I guess," Elizabeth said uncertainly. "But I'm still worried. Things could change."

By the next morning, they already had. The story of Grace being in Bunk Seven's skit was just too good to keep quiet. Practically every girl in the bunk had told at least one person about the great joke they had pulled off. The news that Bunk Seven was hiding an unregistered camper spread rapidly through the camp and soon everyone was buzzing about it. The campers thought it was the best secret and vowed they would all help keep Grace safe.

Many of the girls came by throughout the morning to meet Grace on the sly, and to say they would help protect her from being exposed. Bunk Four and Bunk Two even insisted that she join them as they took a long nature hike in the woods. Although both counselors had noticed her, they each thought that Grace belonged to the other bunk.

"Everyone's being so nice," Grace told Elizabeth after rest hour, as they walked over to the playing field for a soccer game. "That nature hike was terrific. We saw two deer and even a fox."

"It sounds like you're having a great time," Elizabeth said, sincerely happy for her friend.

"And now that I've made so many new friends, I'll kind of spread myself around. That way Bunk Seven won't have to be covering for me all the time."

"Oh, we don't mind," Elizabeth said, "but knowing the other girls will give you a chance to do a lot of different things."

Elizabeth glanced over at Barbara who was standing all alone at the edge of the field. *Were her eyes on Grace?* A baseball cap covered Grace's red curls, but Elizabeth wondered if Barbara had heard the news about Bunk Seven hiding an unregistered camper. Either way, Barbara's presence made Elizabeth nervous.

"Elizabeth," Grace said, "don't you think everyone here is nice?"

Elizabeth wondered if she should share her concerns with Grace. "I'm not so sure," she replied. "Some people may object to us hiding you out."

"What do you mean?" Grace asked worriedly.

Seeing the sudden tension on Grace's face, Elizabeth tried to sound more cheerful. "Oh, never mind. I'm probably just being overly cautious. That's what Jessica always tells me."

But Elizabeth didn't really feel better until the first quarter of the soccer game was over. She looked around for Barbara, but the sullen girl was nowhere to be seen. Elizabeth didn't care where Barbara had disappeared to, as long as she stayed away from Grace.

After the game, Jessica, who had lagged behind to talk to Mrs. Edwards, came running up to Elizabeth who was walking back to the cabin. "Did you hear the news, Lizzie?" she asked.

"What news?"

"We have the rest of the afternoon free to do whatever we want."

Elizabeth looked at Jessica's excited face. "What's so great about that?"

"I have big plans for this afternoon."

Warning bells rang in Elizabeth's head. She knew from experience that Jessica's look of exhilaration meant that she was up to something—something that would most likely land her in hot water. And then, as usual, Elizabeth would have to come to her rescue. "What plans?" Elizabeth asked suspiciously.

Jessica looked up at the sky as she strolled along. "The boys' swim period is in the afternoon. I've seen them out on the float."

"Oh, no," Elizabeth groaned. "You're not

planning to do something about your petition, are you?"

"I sure am," Jessica said, flashing her twin a smile.

"Jess, you know we're not allowed to swim out to the float when the boys are there."

Jessica shrugged. "I'm not planning to swim."

"Then how are you going to get there?"

"I'm taking a canoe."

Elizabeth stopped walking and faced her sister. "Why don't you forget about getting the boys to sign? Just give Mrs. Edwards your petition and see what happens."

"Now why would I want to do that?"

"So you can stay out of trouble," Elizabeth said bluntly.

"Lizzie, if I've said it once, I've said it a hundred times. You worry too much. You were scared about hiding Grace and that's turning out just fine, right?"

"I suppose so," Elizabeth muttered.

"Besides, it'll be fun to see some of the boys from Sweet Valley. Which reminds me, can I borrow your new blue bathing suit?"

Jessica loved borrowing Elizabeth's best clothes, usually before Elizabeth had a chance to wear them herself. "I guess you can," she replied with resignation.

"Thanks." Jessica gave her a bright smile.

Elizabeth tried to reason with her sister one last time. "You know, Jess, it's really unsafe to go out in a canoe by yourself. And I'm not going with you," she added sternly.

"That's all right. I've already thought of the perfect person to help paddle," Jessica replied. "Someone who will never be missed."

"Grace?" Elizabeth asked, having already figured out Jessica's plan.

"Who else?"

Elizabeth decided to spend the rest of her afternoon working on the camp newsletter, and then go horseback riding. But before she began her activities, she walked with Grace and Jessica down to the lake.

"Are you sure you want to do this?" she asked Grace, as the three girls headed down to the water's edge.

"Oh, sure. It's going to be exciting. Won't the boys from Sweet Valley be surprised to see us?"

"They certainly will," Jessica assured her. She put her towel down. "We'd better hurry up, or they'll be gone before we get there."

Elizabeth put her hands on her hips. "Have you thought about what you're going to tell Rose when your canoe gets far away from the others?"

Jessica gave her a superior smile. "I certainly have." She wet her finger and stuck it up. "It's very breezy today, don't you think so, Grace?"

Grace giggled. "It sure is. We might get blown off course."

"I think we might," Jessica said solemnly.

Even Elizabeth had to laugh. "I can see you two have this all figured out. Good luck."

"Thanks, Liz," Jessica said airily. "But we probably won't need it."

Jessica and Grace headed toward a harried Rose who was helping each girl who wanted to take a canoe out on the lake. "Do you have a partner?" Rose said, focusing in on Jessica.

Jessica gestured vaguely toward Grace. "Sure."

"Then go sign out a canoe," Rose said, pointing to a clipboard sitting on a rock. "Set your watch. I want everyone back here in half an hour. Got that?"

Jessica nodded. This was even easier than she thought it would be.

After signing out, Jessica and Grace pushed

the boat into the cool water and started paddling. Grace was not as adept with a paddle as Jessica, but she pulled her weight.

Gradually, the duo moved away from the canoes clustered near Camp Loconda's shore. It took them almost ten minutes, but soon they were close enough to the float to make out a group of boys horsing around.

"There's Bruce Patman," Jessica said, paddling hard. Bruce came from one of the wealthiest families in Sweet Valley, and the Unicorns thought he was the cutest boy in the seventh grade.

"And there's Jerry McAllister," Grace said.

"And there's the counselor," Jessica added, pointing to a tall teenager who was standing on the float. "Luckily he's looking in the other direction."

"What should we do?" Grace asked. "Start paddling back?"

"No way," Jessica said with determination. "Just keep going around in a circle and hope that he leaves."

It took a while, and Grace's arms were getting tired from the constant pulling motions in order to keep the canoe moving, but finally the counselor dove into the water and swam toward shore. That was the girls' cue to paddle as fast as they could to the float.

"Hey, Bruce," Jessica called as they got within shouting distance. "Come over here for a second."

Bruce Patman did a double take. "Jessica Wakefield! What are you doing here?"

The girls paddled closer. "We have something to discuss with you," Jessica said.

Jerry McAllister joined them. "Jessica. And Grace." He leaned over and pulled the canoe as close to the float as possible. Several of the other boys gathered around.

"Is your counselor coming back?" Jessica asked, peering up at her audience.

"No," Bruce replied. "He said we had to come back to shore in five minutes."

"Then I'll hurry." Jessica handed Bruce her petition. "Don't you think it would be a good idea for Camp Loconda and Camp Running Bear to get together and have a dance?"

The boys looked at each other. "I don't know," Bruce said with a shrug. "So far I haven't missed you girls at all."

"That's not very nice," Jessica said with a pout.

A boy they didn't know joined in the conversation. "I'd like to have a dance. After all, what's the point of having girls right across the lake if we never get to see them?"

Jessica and Grace smiled at each other. That was more the response they were looking for.

"What's your name?" Jessica asked, giving him a bright smile.

"Sandy James."

"Well, Sandy, if you help us, there might be a way to have a dance. This is what you have to do. . . ."

Elizabeth had settled down in the arts-and-crafts building where she and several other girls were working on the camp newsletter. As editor of *The Sweet Valley Sixers*, Elizabeth was accustomed to planning and reporting stories. Writing was one of her favorite activities.

"So, let's see," Elizabeth said, opening her notebook and resting it on her lap, "which stories have we decided on?"

Amy, who worked with Elizabeth on *The Sweet Valley Sixers* said, "We definitely want to cover the awards night."

"Yes," a girl named Miriam agreed, "and don't forget to write about the new horse the camp just bought."

"New horse." Elizabeth wrote it down. "And

we'll announce the arts-and-crafts contest. A lot of people will be interested in that."

Alice from Bunk Two leaned back in her wooden chair. "I wish we could have a gossip column."

Elizabeth frowned. "A gossip column? Do we have any good gossip?"

"Sure we do," Alice replied. "We could put something in the column about Grace."

"Grace?" Amy cried. "We don't want to give her away."

"Oh, we wouldn't mention her name or anything," Alice said quickly. "We could just put in a mystery item like, 'What has red hair and turns up at breakfast, lunch, and dinner?'"

"Boy, that would be taking a chance," Elizabeth said. "Maybe if we make the whole column a series of riddles, the counselors will think it's just innocent fun."

"Good idea. But do we have any other gossip?" Amy asked.

"Well, we could say, 'What girl disappears every day and where does she go?'" Miriam said, obviously pleased with her contribution.

"You mean Barbara?" Elizabeth asked. She remembered how Barbara had faded from sight earlier in the morning.

"Yes. I'm in her bunk, and no matter what activities are planned, she just disappears for a couple of hours every day."

"What's her story?" Amy asked. "She sure looks unhappy."

Miriam lowered her voice. "I don't know, but she's weird, especially the way she stares at everybody. One of the girls thinks she is psychic."

Elizabeth made a face. "She's a little strange, but I don't believe that."

Miriam shrugged. "All I know is she gives me the creeps. I don't think anybody likes her and she's already gotten into a few fights with some of the girls in our bunk."

So other people have noticed that Barbara doesn't seem like a very nice person, Elizabeth thought to herself. *It isn't surprising she's unpopular*. Elizabeth doodled Barbara's name in the margin of her notebook. With the news of Grace's presence spreading all over camp, Elizabeth wondered if Barbara knew, and, if so, would she do anything about it.

The newspaper meeting broke up, and Elizabeth and Amy headed toward the stable for a horseback ride.

"I hope the Indian pony is free," Elizabeth said. "He's my favorite."

The first group of riders were just returning

when Elizabeth and Amy got to the stable. The duo was greeted with some exciting news.

"There's going to be a riding competition in a day or two," Nancy called as she dismounted.

Amy smiled. She loved to ride almost as much as Elizabeth did.

"Ooooh, I want to sign up for that," she said. She walked over to her favorite chestnut mare. "I'm going to start practicing now. And so are you," she informed the horse.

After an hour of riding, Elizabeth returned to the cabin. It was late in the afternoon. She found Jessica resting on her bed, reading a magazine.

"Hey," she said, making space on the bed and joining her sister, "how did it go?"

Jessica sat up, her eyes glowing. "It was great. We met this great guy named Sandy who said he'd pass around the petition for us. He was really excited about the dance and he thought plenty of the other guys would be, too."

"Well, that's good," Elizabeth said, relieved that her sister's plan had gone off without any problems—so far, at least. "Where's Grace?"

"She decided to go back to the shack until dinner time. She's coming to the movie with us, too."

"That's right," Elizabeth said. "They're showing a movie tonight."

Jessica leaned back on the bed. "Aren't things perfect, Liz? Grace is having a good time at camp. And thanks to me, there's going to be a super dance."

"I wouldn't get my hopes up about the dance," Elizabeth warned. "A petition doesn't mean approval."

Jessica waved her objections away. "Everything is going according to plan. Just wait and see."

All the campers lined up eagerly at the dining room for a dinner of meat loaf, peas, buttermilk biscuits, and peach pie. Grace had filled her plate with food and was about to join the twins at their table when she felt a hand on her shoulder. She looked up into Jamie's brown eyes.

"Hi," Jamie said in a friendly voice. "I've seen you hanging around with the kids from my bunk, but I don't know your name."

Grace gulped. "Uh, Grace."

"Grace what?"

"Grace Oliver."

A hush fell over the dining room. Everyone could see Grace and Jamie talking, although they couldn't make out any of the words.

"You must know the other girls in my bunk, then," Jamie was saying.

"Oh, I do." Grace turned a pale face toward Jessica who was sitting nearby. Help! her expression clearly read.

"Are you from Sweet Valley?" Jamie continued.

Grace tried to be vague. "I . . . I have a cousin who lives there, so I've met lots of her friends."

"What bunk are you in?" Jamie inquired pleasantly.

Grace didn't know what to say. She kept her eyes on Jessica, whose frantic gestures Grace finally understood. With a slight twist of her body, Grace tipped over her glass of milk, which had been sitting precariously on the edge of her tray. It fell to the floor with a loud crash.

"Gosh, I'm sorry," Grace said, putting down her tray and grabbing a napkin to wipe off the flecks of milk that had spilled on Jamie's arm. Then she knelt down and started to wipe the milk off the floor.

Several girls from other tables ran to Grace's aid, and in the confusion Jamie's question was forgotten. After the mess had been cleaned up, Jamie merely said, "No use crying over spilled milk, right, Grace? Just have fun and I'll see you around."

Heaving a sigh of relief, Grace picked up her tray and marched over to join Jessica, Elizabeth, and a few of the other girls. "That was close," she said, as she took a seat. "Way too close."

"It was great when you spilled the milk, though," Jessica said with admiration.

"Thanks for the idea."

"Do you think Jamie was suspicious?" Elizabeth asked with worry.

"I don't know. She may just have been friendly because she's seen me with you so many times."

"That was probably it," Jessica said reassuringly.

Grace looked around the table at her friends. "I hope so. I'm having such a wonderful time that I would just die if I had to go back home now."

"You won't," Jessica said. "How many close calls could you have in one night?"

After dinner the girls all lined up outside the auditorium for a special showing of *Old Yeller*. Elizabeth loved the book and couldn't wait to see the movie. Everyone was excited.

"Why is everyone moving so slowly?" Jessica

asked as she stood on her tiptoes and tried to see to the front of the line.

"I don't know, but I wish it would move faster," Elizabeth complained. "I want to get a good seat."

Grace left the line to see if she could figure out what was causing the delay. "One of the counselors is stopping people as they go in," she informed them on her return. "Maybe they're giving tickets for door prizes."

But when the trio got near the door, they were horrified to see Tina taking a head count.

"And you said I couldn't have more than one close call in a night," Grace whispered to Jessica.

"Can't you just sneak out of line?" Elizabeth asked.

"It's too late," Jessica replied. "Tina will see her if she leaves. Just go through the line, Grace."

Tina clicked a counter three times as the twins and Grace walked by, and the girls nervously took seats in a back row. A few minutes later, Tina returned to the front of the auditorium.

"You may have seen me using the counter as you came in. We were doing a random head check," she said in her usual gruff tone of voice. "The camp does that to see if anyone is missing. For some reason, I count one extra girl."

Elizabeth closed her eyes.

"I suppose I could have made a mistake, but I'll have to count you again when the movie's over."

Jessica and Grace stared at each other.

"You must have counted me twice," came a voice from the back of the room.

Jessica and Elizabeth gasped. It was Barbara.

Tina looked at her suspiciously. "Why's that?"

"I came into the auditorium, then I went back to the dining room to look for my . . . uh, my sweater." She held it up. "Then I went through the line again."

Tina's face cleared. "Well, that explains it then. Thanks for telling me. You can all go after the movie."

Jessica and Grace heaved a sigh of relief. "Saved," Grace said. "And by Barbara of all people."

Elizabeth turned and looked in Barbara's direction. Several girls close by were discreetly miming applause.

"I guess we owe Barbara one," Jessica said to Elizabeth.

"That's what bothers me," Elizabeth replied. "From everything I've heard about Barbara Fields, she doesn't do things just to be nice."

Jessica pursed her lips. "Well, if she doesn't do favors, that means she's going to want something in return."

Elizabeth sighed. "I have a feeling you're right, Jess. The question is, what?"

Six

◇

As the girls of Bunk Seven got ready for breakfast the next morning, Barbara appeared in the doorway. "My counselor would like to see you, Jamie," she announced.

Jamie looked surprised, but nodded and slipped out the door. There was silence until Jessica walked over to Barbara and said, "I guess we should thank you for getting Grace out of that jam with Tina."

Barbara smiled a superior smile. "Someone had to do something. The rest of you were just sitting there."

Jessica bristled. "We would have thought of something to—"

"But it would have been too late," Barbara interrupted. "Besides, I've decided that hiding Grace is fun."

Elizabeth joined her sister. "You have?"

"Yes. Of course, it's you guys in Bunk Seven who are having the most fun."

The other girls gathered around Barbara. "What do you mean?" Ellen asked.

"Just what I said. You're the ones who are Grace's best friends, and everyone at Camp Loconda thinks you're great for pulling off this stunt." Barbara brushed her hair out of her eyes. "So I've decided I want to be in Bunk Seven, too."

"But you can't," Jessica exploded.

"Why not? After all, there *is* still an empty bed."

Elizabeth and Jessica looked at each other. It was true. Lila's absence did make them one camper short. There was no real reason why Barbara couldn't join their bunk. Except that they didn't want her brooding presence all the time.

"I've already told my counselor that I want to move and that you asked me to come. That's what she's talking to Jamie about right now."

All the girls started talking at the same time. "Hey, you had no right to do that," Nancy said.

"What makes you think we'd even let you?" Kerry added.

"Forget it," Ellen said bluntly.

Barbara's eyes narrowed. "Are you sure that's your decision?" She paused. "Remember how close Grace came to being found out? Well, next time, it could really happen. All someone has to do is leave an anonymous note in Mrs. Edwards' office."

The girls of Bunk Seven looked at each other in horror. So that was Barbara's plan. And the worst part was that Barbara meant every word of it. If they didn't agree to let her in their cabin, she would be mean enough to let the news about Grace slip out.

Elizabeth cleared her throat. "Grace was saying last night how much she wants to stay at camp."

"And we all want her to stay," Nancy said unhappily.

All the girls murmured their assent.

"Well, then," Barbara said, "it's all decided, isn't it?"

"I guess so," Jessica replied, glaring at Barbara.

A couple of the girls shrugged, and Kimberly said, "I don't see that we have a choice."

At that moment, Jamie came back into the room. There was a puzzled look on her face as she said, "I guess you know where I was—and why. I'm just kind of surprised you girls didn't tell me that you wanted Barbara in our bunk."

The awkward silence was broken by Barbara. "We thought it would be better to have the counselors discuss it first," she said. "Is it all right if I stay?"

"I guess so. We do have space and if the girls want you." She turned to the group who unwillingly nodded their heads. "Well, then, it's OK with me."

"Great!" For the first time, what looked like a genuine smile appeared on Barbara's plain face.

"That'll be your bed," Jamie said, pointing to the empty upper bunk in the corner.

"Oh, I don't like to sleep up that high," Barbara said airily. "Who's on the bottom?"

"I am," Nancy said.

"Well, you wouldn't mind changing with me, would you?" It was more of a statement than a question.

Nancy bit her lip. "No," she said, "I wouldn't mind at all."

"Good. I'll go pack my stuff," Barbara said.

As soon as she slammed the door behind her, Jamie faced her group. "I don't understand this, gang. I know Barbara isn't well liked around Camp Loconda. Bunk Three was thrilled that she was leaving. How come you want her with us?"

Elizabeth could tell that Jessica was so angry she was ready to spit out the truth. "Barbara seemed unhappy and she likes us," Elizabeth quickly replied. "We thought it would be a nice thing to do."

"I suppose that's true," Jamie said, looking at her closely. "I just hope she fits in."

After breakfast, Barbara came in with her duffel bag and stashed it under her new bunk. The girls were in the middle of morning bed-making and clean-up. "Here," Jessica said, tossing her a rag. "We have to dust."

Barbara threw the dust rag right back at her. "Hey, I'm not going to be doing any of the chores around here."

Jessica glared at her. "Why not?"

"Because I don't want to," Barbara said defiantly. Her message was clear. She was calling the shots now, and the other girls would have to put up with her or suffer the consequences.

That afternoon the campers were informed

that dinner would have a Hawaiian theme, and
that the bunk who came up with the best costumes would earn an extra treat at supper.

"What should we go as?" Elizabeth asked.

"Everyone will probably be dressed as hula
dancers," Jessica said. "So we'll need to do something really special to make our hula costumes
better."

"What about actually doing a hula dance?"
Nancy suggested. "We could get a cassette player
and tape from the rec room, and then we could
surprise everyone once they're ready to start eating."

"That's a great idea," Kimberly said enthusiastically.

"We can all wear our bathing suit tops and we
can use crepe paper to make the skirts."

Barbara, who was lying on her bed reading,
spoke up. "I think wearing bathing suit tops and
paper skirts and doing a hula dance is silly," she
commented without looking up.

"Well, do you have a better idea?" Nancy
asked angrily.

"I'd rather be a clown."

The girls looked at each other blankly. "But
that has nothing to do with the dinner theme,"

Elizabeth pointed out. "We won't have a chance of winning."

Barbara shrugged. "So what? I want to be a clown, and if you don't agree, well, just remember Grace."

All the girls were upset by Barbara's threat, but there was not much they could do about it, so for the rest of the afternoon they tried to put clown costumes together. They mismatched their clothes and smeared their faces with grease pencils they found in the arts-and-crafts building. At dinner time, the other campers looked at them curiously as they entered the dining hall. Every girl, except those in Bunk Seven, had come dressed for a luau. Bunk Two had added an extra touch to their hula costumes by wearing crowns of wildflowers on their heads. They won the prize—a basketful of pineapples.

By the end of dinner, the other campers were aware of what Barbara was up to and they too were forced to put up with her bossy ways. After all, Barbara was holding Grace's future in her hand. Since everyone liked Grace and wanted her to stay, they would have to do whatever Barbara said. And, it wasn't going to be easy.

If there was a line, Barbara went to the head of

it. If there was a team game, she became captain. When candy apples were handed out as a special treat at lunch, Barbara demanded that several girls give her theirs. The only time she made no demands was when she routinely disappeared in the middle of the day.

"I wonder where she goes," Jessica said. Girls from several different bunks, along with Elizabeth, Amy, and Grace were lounging in the meadow behind the stable.

"Who cares?" Nancy said. "I just wish she'd disappear and never come back."

"There're all kinds of rumors about Barbara, you know," one of the other girls said.

"That's right," Jessica confirmed. "I've heard she goes off to do some kind of weird magic."

Amy made a face. "I agree she's pretty awful, but I don't believe that. If she was any good at magic, she would conjure up a few friends."

Jessica pulled a leaf off a tree. "She's good at making herself disappear, though."

Grace sat picking at the grass, a troubled look on her face. "You know, I feel terrible about this. Everyone was having such a good time until I came along. Now everything is ruined—because of me!"

All the girls tried to reassure Grace that it was not her fault.

"We want you here, Grace."

"We'll just have to put up with Barbara."

"Thanks," Grace said gratefully.

"Does she boss you around," Elizabeth asked, "like she does the rest of us?"

Grace got an embarrassed look on her face. "Actually, she's pretty nice to me. She always acts like we're pals. As if we have something in common."

"Well, that's good, anyway," Elizabeth said sensibly. "If she likes you, maybe she won't tell."

Grace sighed. "I wish we could count on that."

One thing that raised Bunk Seven's spirits was their scheduled overnight canoe trip. It wouldn't be long now before it was their bunk's turn to paddle to the other side of the lake. In a few hours they'd be pitching their tents for the night.

As they were packing to go, Grace came by the cabin to say goodbye.

"I wish you were going with us," Elizabeth said as she stuffed her bathing suit into her duffel bag.

"Me, too, but you'll have fun, anyway."

"You bet," Jessica declared as she threw her toothbrush into her bag.

"I doubt it," Barbara grumbled from her bed. "Sleeping on the hard ground is no fun."

The girls of Bunk Seven looked at each other in horror. Barbara wasn't going to say they couldn't go, was she?

But Barbara just looked at them with a superior smile. "Don't worry. It would be too suspicious if we missed our turn."

"Gee, thanks a lot, Barbara," Jessica said bitterly.

All the hard feelings were forgotten when the girls set off in their canoes to the site across the lake. The weather was perfect for canoeing, with just enough breeze to help them to their destination. Even Barbara seemed to be enjoying herself as she took her turn paddling.

"Is this the spot?" Elizabeth asked, as they dragged their canoes onto the shore.

Jamie smiled. "Nope, we have to hike a bit to get there. Grab your gear and let's get going."

The girls grumbled a little as they made their way through the woods, but they had fun identifying flowers and trees, and they even saw a deer looking for food.

"Here we are," Jamie finally declared.

They had arrived at a clearing with a stone fireplace in the middle. Enthusiastically, the girls began pitching the tents. Their spirits were so high, they didn't even mind doing Barbara's share of the work after she claimed to have hurt her ankle on the hike.

Jamie pointed at Elizabeth, Jessica, and Amy. "Why don't you three start collecting some firewood, but don't go too far."

The trio set off happily, picking up usable pieces of wood, and tossing aside those that were too green.

"Hey, what's that noise?" Amy said, looking up from her search.

"Come on, Amy. This isn't a rerun of Crying Moon and Running Bear, is it?" Jessica asked.

"No. I heard a noise. Like a moan."

"Maybe someone's hurt," Elizabeth said with concern.

"Well, I suppose we could look around," Jessica said uncertainly.

"All right. But let's stay within sight of each other."

The girls spread out a little. "Is anyone there?" Elizabeth called.

Another moan answered them, and this time all the girls heard it.

"Is anyone there?" Amy asked, raising her voice.

But now all was quiet.

"I think it came from that direction," Amy said pointing.

The girls ventured a little further into the woods, staying close together, but they couldn't find anything that might have made the noise.

"Hey, what are you three doing?" Nancy stood a few feet away from them, her hands on her hips.

"We thought we heard something," Jessica explained.

"A moan."

Nancy frowned. "Well, Jamie is getting worried about you. You'd better come back to camp."

When the girls returned, they tried to explain about the moaning, but Jamie waved away their concern. "Some animals sound a great deal like humans. If you looked and didn't find anything, I'm sure nothing was wrong. Now let's get these hot dogs ready for the fire."

Dusk was falling and the girls gathered around the campfire to cook their hot dogs. There was laughter and joking as Jamie told them a funny story.

By the time they had finished roasting their marshmallows, the girls were tired from their day.

"You know, it's such a nice night," Jamie said, looking up at the stars. "We don't have to sleep inside our tents."

"You mean we can sleep around the campfire?" Jessica said with excitement.

"Sure, if you want to."

"Well, I don't," Barbara declared. She gathered up her things and headed for her tent.

"I guess I don't, either," Nancy said reluctantly.

In the end, only Jessica, Elizabeth, Ellen, and Amy chose to sleep outside.

"Have a good night's sleep, you all," Jamie said as she herself took shelter inside her tent and pulled down the front flap.

"I hope it's a quiet one," Amy muttered as she tried to find a comfortable spot to unfold her sleeping bag.

"Oh, don't worry," Jessica said. "We were out in the woods when we heard that noise. We won't hear it again."

The words were hardly out of Jessica's mouth when a low moan drifted to them on the wind.

"Did you hear that?" Elizabeth asked in a quavery voice.

"No," Jessica said. "At least I'm going to pretend I didn't."

"It's probably an animal, just like Jamie said," Ellen reminded them.

Amy sat up in a panic. "An animal?"

Elizabeth rolled over and looked at her friend. "We don't want to go back inside our tents yet, Amy. The others would say we're babies.

"I guess so." Amy laid back down.

All was quiet for a few moments. Then another sound broke the silence. This time it sounded more like a groan.

"Can we go in now?" Amy asked.

"Let's just wait a few minutes," Jessica insisted, closing her eyes.

"Hey, is it raining?" Ellen asked.

"What do you mean?" Elizabeth demanded. Then she, too, felt sprinkles on her face.

Jessica raised herself on one arm. "I felt it, too." She looked up at the starry sky. "But there isn't even a visible cloud."

"What's going on here?" Elizabeth asked with a frown, as more water rained down on her face.

Another moaning sound was heard, but it was broken by a snort of laughter.

"Hey, who's out there?" Jessica hissed.

From out of the woods, pushing each other and laughing, ran Bruce Patman, Aaron Dallas, Jerry McAllister, and Sandy James. Each of them held water pistols in their hands.

"What are you doing here?" Elizabeth demanded, as she sat up.

Jessica rolled her eyes. "You guys are crazy!"

"We heard your bunk was going to be spending an overnight here," Jerry said, "and we thought we'd welcome you."

"Welcome," Amy sputtered. "You nearly scared us to death."

"Well, that was the general idea." Bruce laughed.

Aaron moaned in the way that was now familiar to them and pointed his water pistol in their direction.

Ellen scooted further down in her sleeping bag. "Aaron Dallas, don't you dare!"

Before Aaron could take aim and fire, Jamie marched out of the tent. "What's going on here?"

"Uh, nothing," Bruce said.

"Does your counselor know you're here?" Jamie demanded.

The boys stood silent.

"I think it's time you got back to your camp, don't you?" Jamie asked.

"I guess so," Jerry said, scuffing his toe against the ground.

Aaron, Bruce, and Jerry turned to leave, but Sandy came up to Jessica and handed her an envelope. "Here you go, Jessica. Signed, sealed, and delivered." Then he followed his friends.

"Did you know those boys were coming to our campsite?" Jamie asked.

"No," Jessica said.

"They were just trying to scare us," Elizabeth explained.

Jamie looked at the envelope in Jessica's hand. "I could ask you to show me what's inside, but I guess it's private property."

Jessica didn't say a word, but hoped she looked innocent.

Jamie hesitated for a moment, then turned toward the tent. "I don't want to hear another sound from out here."

"You won't," Ellen assured her, and Jamie seemed satisfied as she went back to bed.

The moment Jamie was out of sight, Jessica opened the envelope. Out fluttered three pages of the petition, all signed with the names of Camp Running Bear campers. "All right!" she cheered quietly.

"I guess Sandy really wanted to get this to you, considering the chance he took," Elizabeth said.

"I don't see how Mrs. Edwards can refuse when we have this kind of response to our dance," Jessica said with satisfaction.

"Me, either," Ellen agreed, looking down the list of names.

"How are you going to tell Mrs. Edwards that we want this dance, Jess?" Elizabeth wanted to know.

"I don't know yet," Jessica answered thoughtfully. "But it's got to be something impressive so she won't be able to say no."

Elizabeth smiled. Jessica had gotten this far with her petition. She was sure her twin would come up with a scheme to persuade Mrs. Edwards that a dance with the boys' camp was a great idea.

Seven

◇

"Up and at 'em," Jamie called from the tent the next morning. "It's time to get going if we want to be back in time to play capture the flag."

Jessica jumped out of her sleeping bag. She didn't want to miss the fun.

As the girls gobbled down their breakfast, they excitedly discussed the morning's activity. It was going to be a real war!

"How does it work? I've heard people talking about it, but I don't know how you play," Amy said as she packed the utensils away.

"The camp is divided into two teams," Jessica explained. "We're each given a flag—"

"A towel in this case," Jamie interrupted, looking up from her cleaning.

"And it gets put someplace where the opposing team can't get at it very easily," Jessica finished.

"Like in a tree branch," Elizabeth interjected.

Amy looked excited. "Then what?"

"The object is to capture your opponents' flag and bring it back to your territory," Jamie said.

"It's not easy," Elizabeth added, "since the other team is trying to tag you out."

"Sounds like fun," Amy said.

"Sounds stupid to me," Barbara muttered as she kicked some dirt onto the campfire spot.

Jessica looked around to see if Jamie was still within earshot. "You'd better not ruin this for us," she hissed.

Barbara just shrugged.

By the time Bunk Seven arrived back at camp and docked their canoes, the preparations for capture the flag were underway. Mrs. Edwards was placing a pink streamer down the center of the grass field, dividing it into two enemy territories. Tina was passing out red and blue bandanas to the girls that would denote the two teams. Bunk Seven was on the Red Team.

Talking and laughing excitedly, the girls milled around waiting for the game to begin. When Mrs. Edwards placed a red towel and a blue towel in tree branches at each end of the field, they knew the starting whistle would be blowing soon.

"Does everyone understand the rules?" Mrs. Edwards called from the center of the field.

All the girls cheered and said yes.

"Then line up," Mrs. Edwards said.

With girls lined up on either side of the pink streamer, Mrs. Edwards blew her whistle and the mad scramble began.

Campers dashed everywhere as they tried to avoid being tagged by members of the other team. At the same time, they tried to make a few tags of their own to eliminate their rivals.

Jessica had a close call as she barreled toward the Blue Team's flag. Out of nowhere, one of the rival girls came within inches of her. If Jessica hadn't moved her arm, she would have been tagged out of the game.

"I just had a close call," Jessica said, as she passed one of her Red teammates. One thing about capture the flag—you had to be on the lookout at all times.

Some of the girls from Bunk Seven were not

as fortunate as Jessica. Kerry and Kimberly were bumped by rushing Blue Team members, and they had to leave the field. Then Nancy stumbled and fell, giving two girls the chance to tag her out. But Elizabeth bypassed several Blue Team members, and Ellen and Amy did even better, each tagging two of their opponents out of the game. Even Barbara stayed on her feet, managing a tag of her own.

After some hard moments of play, Jessica screamed as she looked over her shoulder. "Oh, no! They got our flag!"

Sure enough, one of the girls from the Blue Team was proudly waving the red flag. Now the Red Team had to prevent the Blues from getting back to their own territory. And, of course, they still had to steal the Blue Team's flag.

Jessica wasn't about to lose without a fight. She sprinted to the tree from which the blue flag was hanging. With a small jump she reached up and grabbed the flag. "I've got it, I've got it!" she yelled.

She turned and began to run back toward the safety of her own territory. The Blue Team members who were left on the field charged after her.

Jessica looked around. She had to toss the flag

to one of her teammates because she was in danger of being tagged out. Elizabeth and most of the other girls were down at the other end of the field defending the Red Team's flag. There was no way she could reach them. The Blues came closer and closer, surrounding her. She had to get rid of the flag right now!

"Oh, no," Jessica moaned. There was a Red Team member within throwing distance, but it was Barbara. With no other choice, Jessica lifted her arm and threw the flag to Barbara.

Barbara caught it deftly in one hand and continued running toward the Red Team's territory. She was about to cross the line, when the flag flew out of her hand and landed on the ground.

Almost immediately, a Blue Team member picked up the flag and ran back to place it on the tree limb where the Reds would have to get it down again.

It was all over for the Red Team. They could not hope to get close to the blue flag and keep members of the Blue Team, who were whooping and shouting with the red flag in hand, from reaching their own side. The members of the Blue Team crossed over to their own territory and held their opponents' flag aloft triumphantly. Mrs.

Edwards blew her whistle. "The Blue Team wins!" she shouted.

The Red Team good-naturedly shook the winners' hands, but Jessica was angry. "Hey, Barbara," she said as they walked back to the bunk. "You dropped our flag on purpose, didn't you?"

"What's the difference?" Barbara said, not answering the question.

"Then you did!" Jessica said accusingly.

Barbara shrugged. "Think whatever you like. I couldn't care less." Then she walked away.

"She's responsible for our losing," Jessica grumbled.

"Come on, Jess, it may have been an accident," Elizabeth said.

"We lost now, anyway," Amy added. "And that's that."

"Let's not think about it anymore," Elizabeth said as they watched Barbara's receding figure. "It's lunchtime and I'm hungry."

"Then there's the horseback riding competition," Amy remembered.

After they had eaten their sandwiches and chips, the girls in Bunk Seven went over to the stable. Grace, a drawing pad and pencil in her hand, met them there.

"Are you going to ride today, Grace?" Elizabeth asked.

"No, I don't want to call too much attention to myself."

"What's the pad for?" Jessica wanted to know.

"I've gotten into drawing horses lately," Grace said with a smile.

Jessica made a face. "Well, don't draw me while I'm in the ring. I'm not sure I want to see what I look like out there."

Lee, the riding instructor, was organizing the riding contest. "Listen up, everyone. I'm going to give you points for ability to handle your horse, your posture, the position of your feet, and how well you execute the commands," she said.

Elizabeth, along with several of the other campers at her level of expertise, saddled up and then entered the ring. She was riding Joy, the spotted Indian pony she had fallen in love with her first day at camp.

After walking once around the ring, Lee told the girls to trot from a posting position. Elizabeth felt confident as she lifted herself up from the saddle.

Next the girls trotted from a sitting position.

Amy bounced uncomfortably because her feet had come out of the stirrups.

Finally, Lee asked for a slow canter. That was the most difficult for Elizabeth. She often had trouble keeping her balance as her horse lunged forward. But today, everything went smoothly. Elizabeth felt that she had done a good job.

"Lizzie, you were terrific," Jessica said enthusiastically, as Elizabeth rejoined her bunkmates.

"Thanks."

Amy tilted her head in Lee's direction. "I think she's having a hard time with the judging."

"Well, there's so much to think about," Grace commented.

"You're telling me," Elizabeth said as they waited for Lee to make her decision. Finally, she came to the center of the ring.

"I think everyone did a nice job, but we can only have one winner in this group." She paused dramatically. "And that winner is Elizabeth Wakefield."

Elizabeth gave a little scream and all her friends patted her on the back.

"Elizabeth, please come up and get your trophy."

With a grin on her face, Elizabeth walked to

the center of the ring, and took the small silver-colored cup that Lee handed her.

"Thank you," Elizabeth said, "but there's someone I should share this with." She walked over to Joy and patted her on the head. Then she reached into her pocket and pulled out a few sugar cubes and gave them to the eager horse.

"That was really exciting," Grace said. She and Elizabeth watched the next set of competing riders, then walked back to the bunk so Elizabeth could put her trophy on her dresser.

"Don't forget to put your name in the camp newsletter along with the other winners," Grace said. "Why don't you list it first?"

"That wouldn't be very modest." Elizabeth grinned. "But maybe I'll do it anyway."

"Good for you. What about the arts-and-crafts contest? Are you going to write that up, too?"

"Of course," Elizabeth replied. "Everyone is really excited about it."

"I know I can't be in the contest, but I love the class. I'm working on a horse statue."

"I'd love to see it," Elizabeth said. "Can you show it to me now?"

The arts-and-crafts room was a hub of activity

when Elizabeth and Grace entered it. Many of the girls were readying their entries for the contest. As Elizabeth walked through the room, she could see a towering ice-cream stick castle that one girl was constructing. Another was working on a pottery bowl done in an Indian style.

"There are some pretty impressive entries here," Elizabeth said, stopping to look more carefully at a metal sculpture someone had left on the table.

"I know." A shadow passed over Grace's face.

"You wish yours could be in the show, don't you?" Elizabeth asked sympathetically.

Grace nodded. Then she brightened. "It doesn't really matter as long as I get to be here."

"Well, let's see your statue."

Grace hurried to the large closet that held a number of projects. Reaching up to a high shelf, she brought down a clay statue of a horse. But it was more than a horse, it was a perfectly executed replica of Brownie, Grace's favorite horse at the stable.

"Grace, it's wonderful!" Elizabeth exclaimed.

"Do you really think so?"

Elizabeth took the statue in her hand and turned it over, examining it from every angle. "I certainly do. This is very professional."

"I do go to art classes in Sweet Valley, and of course I draw a lot, but this is the first time I've ever tried something so difficult."

"How did you make it look like Brownie?"

"First I drew some sketches of him, then I worked it out in clay."

Elizabeth carefully handed the statue back to Grace. "Well, I can certainly see why you want it in the show. It would be a prizewinner for sure."

"Thanks, Elizabeth. Uh-oh," she said, her gaze landing on someone coming into the arts-and-crafts room. "Look who's here."

Elizabeth knew immediately who Grace meant. She turned to see Barbara walking up to them.

"What have you got there?" she asked, eyeing the horse statue in Grace's hand.

"Oh, just something I've been working on," Grace mumbled. Barbara looked the sculpture over carefully. "This is really good," she said, the admiration plain in her voice.

"Thanks," Grace muttered.

"It's too bad you can't enter it in the arts-and-crafts contest," Barbara said thoughtfully.

Elizabeth stood nervously. She didn't like the way Barbara was looking at the sculpture.

"When is the judging?" Barbara inquired.

"Before tonight's campfire," Grace said. "All entries will be set up outside on a table where everyone can look at them. Then Mrs. Edwards and Blair, the arts-and-crafts counselor, will judge them and decide who gets the trophies."

"This certainly looks like a winner. Too bad it can't be in the contest. Well, bye," Barbara said abruptly, before moving to another part of the room.

Grace carefully placed the statue back in the closet. "I think I'm going to go back up to the hill," she said sadly.

"Don't you want to hang around our bunk for a while? We could play cards," Elizabeth suggested. She didn't want Grace to go off by herself when she looked so unhappy.

Grace forced a smile. "No, that's all right. I want to be alone for a while. I'll see you at dinner."

"OK," Elizabeth said, trying to sound upbeat. "Jessica will probably come up with a surefire plan to present the dance petition by then."

Now Grace's grin was genuine. "Well, I certainly wouldn't want to miss that."

*   *   *

By the time Grace showed up at the dining room for dinner, Jessica was indeed getting ready to present the petition to Mrs. Edwards.

"What did I miss?" Grace said, slipping into a seat.

"Not much," Jessica smiled. "I was just saying I think we should all stand up and hand it to her."

"You mean all of Bunk Seven?"

"No, I mean the whole camp!"

"Well, that would be impressive," Grace laughed. "Is the petition in there?" she asked, pointing to a blue folder.

"Yes, doesn't it look great?" Jessica replied with satisfaction. She had hand-painted the cover in arts and crafts, decorating it with the word "DANCE" in different colors.

"So when do you think we should present the petition?" Elizabeth asked.

Before Jessica could answer, Barbara came out of the dinner line and headed to Bunk Seven's table. "What are you talking about?" she demanded as she took a seat.

Elizabeth frowned, but quickly filled Barbara in about the plans to have a boy-girl dance.

"A dance? I don't want to have a dance," Barbara said, taking a bite of her hamburger.

Jessica stared at her incredulously. "Who cares if you don't want a dance?"

"Nobody said you have to come," Ellen said pointedly.

"That's for sure," Kimberly muttered.

Barbara ignored all their comments. "Forget it. I hate boy-girl parties, so that's that."

"What do you mean?" Jessica exclaimed.

Barbara wiped her mouth slowly with her napkin before answering. "Could you really have a good time at the party if Grace weren't there?"

Grace grew red, then hung her head. A silence hung over the table like a black cloud. Only Barbara seemed immune to the bad feelings that were swirling around. She finished her dinner in silence, ignoring the dirty looks that were coming her way. The moment she picked up her tray and left the table, there was an explosion of angry words.

"I could kill her," Jessica burst out. "After I worked so hard on this idea."

Ellen nodded. "She's ruined everything."

"No, she hasn't," Grace burst in. "I'm the one who's ruined everything."

"That's not true, Grace," Elizabeth said, patting her friend's shoulder.

Tears welled up in Grace's eyes. "Yes, it is," she insisted.

The girls spent the rest of the meal comforting Grace. Finally, Elizabeth said, "Grace, you wanted to see the judging of the arts-and-crafts show, didn't you?"

Grace nodded.

"Well, it's just about to begin. We've all finished eating, so we might as well go and take a look."

It was a lovely summer night, with plenty of light to see the entries laid out on the card tables. Mrs. Edwards and some of the other counselors were talking with the campers as they walked around, viewing the artwork.

"This one is nice," Grace said, pointing to a woven basket.

Elizabeth was looking at a ceramic pot when something at another table caught her eye. She clutched Grace's arm. "Grace, look over there. Isn't that your horse?"

Grace's eyes widened. "Oh, no. Do you think they could have put it out by mistake?"

Hurrying over to the statue, Elizabeth picked up the tag attached to the foot of the horse. "I don't believe this," she cried.

"What is it?" Grace asked.

Elizabeth flipped the tag over so Grace could see. "Take a look for yourself. This piece was entered by Barbara Fields!"

Eight

◇

Grace grew pale as she held the tag in her hand. "I don't believe it," she said.

Elizabeth looked around the group of campers milling about. "Where is she? I want to give her a piece of my mind."

Grace put a hand on Elizabeth's shoulder. "No, don't. It would just call attention to me."

Elizabeth took a few deep breaths. "You're right, I guess, but I don't see how she could have the nerve to do it. Pretending the statue was made by her is the lowest thing I can think of.

"Shh," Grace said, turning her eyes toward the judges who were making their way to the table. "There's Mrs. Edwards. Don't let her know what's going on."

The girls stepped back while the judges examined each piece on the table. When they came to Grace's horse, Mrs. Edwards picked it up and smiled. After looking it over carefully, she handed it to the arts-and-crafts counselor, who pointed out some of the more detailed work on the horse's legs. There was some more conversation, then Mrs. Edwards placed a blue ribbon on the statue of Brownie.

"Oh, Grace, you've won," Elizabeth cried.

"And no one will ever know it," Grace said bitterly.

"I wouldn't be too sure of that." Elizabeth put her arm around Grace's shoulder.

Several of the other campers came over to see why Grace was so upset, and soon word spread around the group that Barbara was taking credit for Grace's statue.

As the rumbling grew, Grace turned to Elizabeth and said, "Is everyone talking about me?"

"Don't worry, they're all on your side."

"I wish everyone would just forget about it," Grace said.

Elizabeth put her finger to her lips. "Mrs.

Edwards is about to make the announcement right now."

Mrs. Edwards was clapping her hands together for attention. "Campers, I want to say that this is one of the best arts-and-crafts shows we've ever had at Camp Loconda."

All the girls applauded, but most of them looked with sympathy in Grace's direction.

"Now I'd like to announce the names of the winners."

Accompanied by the applause of the crowd, the third- and second-place contestants came up and received the trophies that went along with the ribbons. Then Mrs. Edwards held up the beautiful statue of Brownie.

Jessica, who had just come into the judging area said, "That looks just like your horse, Grace. The one that Elizabeth was describing to me."

"Yes, but look who's taking the blue ribbon for it," Elizabeth said.

"The winner is Barbara Fields," Mrs. Edwards announced.

Barbara appeared at Mrs. Edwards' side. "Well, Barbara, this is a wonderful piece of artwork. You really deserve first place."

"Thank you," Barbara said modestly. Only one or two campers applauded.

After the trophy was given, the crowd quickly dispersed. "Barbara hasn't heard the last about this!" Jessica declared.

Grace and Elizabeth tried to restrain her, but Jessica marched right up to Barbara.

"How could you do that?" Jessica demanded.

"But I was going—"

"Taking Grace's statue of Brownie and pretending it was your own—just because you don't have any talent," Jessica fumed.

"You think you're so smart, don't you? Well, for your information—"

"Don't even try to explain," Jessica interrupted again. "And if everyone didn't like Grace so much, we would do the smart thing and tell you to get lost."

"That's right. How does it feel to know the only way you can get people to pay any attention to you is by blackmailing them?" Elizabeth chimed in.

Barbara's face took on its usual hard look. "That's too bad, isn't it? I'm still in charge, and right now what I want you to do is leave me alone." With that she marched off, trophy in hand.

"Ooh, I could just kill her," Jessica exclaimed.

Grace sat down under a pine tree. "This is turning into a gigantic mess," she said.

The twins sat down next to her. "Oh, it's not so bad," Elizabeth said.

"We'll find a way to deal with her," Jessica said, trying to comfort Grace.

"If I hadn't shown up here, everyone would be having a terrific time at camp. Now you're all under Barbara's thumb, giving in to her every demand, just because you don't want me to be found out."

"But we want you here," Elizabeth said loyally.

Jessica nodded. "Of course we do."

Grace picked up a pinecone and rubbed her thumb across its ridges. "The best thing would be for me to leave."

"Oh, don't say that," Elizabeth protested. She patted Grace's hand. "Jessica's right. We'll find a way to handle Barbara. Maybe I can make her see how awful she's being."

"I doubt that," Grace said with a deep sigh. "As long as I'm around, there's no reason she should change her attitude."

Jessica and Elizabeth exchanged a glance. It was true; Grace was making perfect sense. But to have her leave was unthinkable.

Elizabeth tried once more to make her feel

better. "You know, Grace, everyone thinks hiding you here at camp is really fun."

"Maybe they thought that in the beginning," Grace corrected, "but now they think I'm just a big pain." And before Jessica or Elizabeth could say another word, Grace got up and ran toward the shack on the hill.

Jessica started to go after her, but Elizabeth put a hand on her shoulder. "Let her go," she said. "I think she just needs to be alone for a while."

"Maybe you're right. I guess we can talk to her when she comes back for the campfire."

The nightly campfires were Elizabeth's favorite part of the day. All of the campers were relaxed after a long, active day and a good supper and Elizabeth enjoyed having the chance to get to know some of the other girls.

As she watched the campers gathering, Elizabeth noticed that Grace was not there. "Should I go up and get her?" Jessica asked, glancing up at the hill.

"Why don't we leave her alone for the night," Elizabeth said. "Tomorrow we'll tell her it doesn't matter about Barbara. We want her with us anyway."

After a few songs, the campers were ready for

the skit Bunk One had prepared. It was going to have an outer space theme and everyone was eager to see it. But before they were called to start, Mrs. Edwards got up to speak.

"It has come to my attention, campers, that you girls have made your own arrangements to hold a dance with the boys from Running Bear."

Jessica and Elizabeth looked at each other in amazement.

Mrs. Edwards shook her head. "Why haven't I heard about this from you? Jessica Wakefield, I understand you have something to do with this."

Slowly, Jessica rose to her feet. "Well, uh, yes. Having a dance with the boys was my idea."

"And I think it's a very good one."

"You do?"

"Yes. After you mentioned your idea to me, when camp first started, I decided I would take your suggestion. But I'm afraid I got so busy I just never got around to it. Then when I heard about the petition—"

Jessica cleared her throat. "Excuse me, Mrs. Edwards, but how did you hear about it?"

"The boys kept asking when the dance was going to be. You see, they told their counselors all about the petition and they in turn called and asked me when it was scheduled."

Jessica nodded. She had never told the boys to keep the dance a secret.

"Of course, you should not have paddled over there while the boys were swimming," Mrs. Edwards added, her voice stern. "Still, it was rather clever," she added with a smile.

"Thank you," Jessica said, relieved that she was getting off the hook so easily.

"So when were you planning on letting me in on your little secret?"

Jessica shot a dirty look in Barbara's direction, but kept her words vague. "Oh, we were just waiting until the right time."

"No time like the present, I always say. Since we all like the idea, and the boys do, too, I've arranged to have the dance the day before camp ends. Will that do?"

All the girls applauded and cheered.

The next morning Bunk Seven—all except Barbara, who had made her bed and left before the others had gotten up—was still talking about the upcoming dance as they got ready for breakfast.

Nancy was digging through her duffel bag, throwing shorts and shirts onto the bed. "I don't have a thing to wear," she wailed.

Kimberly, who was examining her wardrobe a

little more carefully, agreed. "I never expected a dance, so I didn't bring anything special to wear."

"We might have to pool our stuff," Jessica said, coming over to look at Kimberly's meager pile of clothes. She picked up a red-and-white-striped blouse. "I have some new white shorts you can borrow that would go with this."

"You do?" Kimberly said gratefully. "Take a look through my stuff and see if there's anything there for you."

Soon all the girls were happily trying on one another's clothing. Elizabeth borrowed a blue sleeveless blouse from Nancy. Jessica took Ellen's jean skirt and paired it with her own yellow T-shirt. "Can I wear your yellow barrettes, Lizzie?" she called.

Elizabeth shrugged. She was used to Jessica borrowing her best things, but everyone trading back and forth like this was more fun than just loaning things to Jessica. The girls were giggling and modeling their new finery when Barbara appeared in the doorway, her expression darker than usual.

Slowly, the laughter faded. Barbara's presence hung like a black cloud, ready to rain on the girls' parade.

"Here," she said, coming over to Elizabeth and shoving an envelope into her hand. "This was left for you."

"What is it?" Elizabeth said, examining it.

Barbara shrugged. "I don't know. I think it's from Grace."

"Grace! Where did you find it?"

"It doesn't matter. I just saw your name on it and decided to bring it to you.

Before Elizabeth, or the others, could question Barbara further, Jamie appeared at the door. Her jaw dropped as she looked around the room. "Did a cyclone just hit this place?"

Elizabeth looked around. Clothes were strewn everywhere. The belongings of each bunk member had been pawed through, and, except for the most desirable items, flung aside. Now the clothing lay in heaps on the beds and on the floor.

"We were looking for stuff to wear to the dance," Jessica explained.

"I hope you found something," Jamie said grimly, "because now it's time to put all this back. And I mean now!"

Jamie's tone meant there was no arguing, and the girls quickly put their things away. Barbara sat on her bed watching. When everything was cleared and the beds made, Jamie said, "All right, let's get to breakfast. If there's anything left."

Silently, the girls walked out into the cool morning air and headed toward the dining room. Elizabeth hung behind the others to read Grace's note.

DEAR ELIZABETH,
I'VE DECIDED TO GO TO MY GODMOTHER'S HOUSE. IT'S NOT FAIR FOR YOU TO HAVE TO PUT UP WITH BARBARA JUST BECAUSE OF ME. CAMP'S BEEN TERRIFIC. PLEASE TELL JESSICA AND THE OTHERS HOW GREAT THEY'VE BEEN TO ME. I'LL SEE YOU BACK IN SWEET VALLEY. LOVE, GRACE.

Elizabeth bit her lip. She suspected the note would be from Grace, but she had hoped she would have a chance to stop her.

"Jessica," she called to her twin, who turned at the urgency in Elizabeth's voice. "Come here."

Jessica hurried over and read the note Elizabeth handed her.

"That Barbara," Jessica exploded.

"Maybe Grace hasn't left yet," Elizabeth said, looking up toward the cabin on the hill.

Jessica followed her gaze. "We could go see. I don't think anyone would miss us at breakfast."

"Jamie would," Elizabeth said glumly.

"Let's tell her I lost my bracelet near the campfire and maybe she'll let us go look."

"Good idea," Elizabeth agreed. They caught up to Jamie and asked permission to skip breakfast.

While the others went off to the dining room, the twins circled back behind the administration building as though they were going to the campfire site. Then they headed up the hill.

"At least we can see where we're going this time," Jessica said, huffing and puffing.

"I don't like the look of that sky, though," Elizabeth replied, pointing to threatening rain clouds that were appearing in the west. "It looks like it's going to pour."

"You're right," Jessica agreed, stumbling a little over a rock in the path. "I hope Grace decided to stay put."

But when the girls got to the shack and knocked on the door, there was no reply. Even in the daylight, the deserted hut was a little scary-looking. Elizabeth hesitated before opening the door but she finally flung it wide. The room was silent and empty.

It didn't take long to do a complete check of the cabin, confirming what the girls suspected. Grace was gone.

"Now what?" Elizabeth said, sitting heavily on the bed.

Jessica glanced out the window to check on the storm clouds that were gathering quickly. "Let's get back to camp and discuss it there. I don't want to get caught in the rain."

Running down the hill under the inky sky, the girls made it back to Camp Loconda in about half the time it had taken them to climb up the hill. Elizabeth stopped to catch her breath. "We're supposed to have horseback riding this morning but they've probably canceled it with the storm coming."

"Let's go back to the bunk and see if the girls are there."

All of Bunk Seven, except Barbara, was waiting for them. "Where have you been?" the cry went up.

"How come you just disappeared like that?" Ellen demanded.

"Did it have something to do with that note?" Amy wanted to know.

Quickly, they filled the girls in on Grace's disappearance.

"Well, it's probably all right," Nancy said. "She had enough money to get to her godmother's house, didn't she?"

"I'm sure she did," Elizabeth replied, "but it's a long walk to the bus station. And the weather is getting worse by the minute." Raindrops were already whipping against the cabin windows.

"There was a storm warning," Kimberly said worriedly. "That's why all outdoor activities are canceled."

"If only we knew how long ago she left," Jessica said, staring out the window with concern. "Then we could figure out if she's at the bus station already."

"You know," Elizabeth said slowly, "we could call and see if she's there."

"Call?" Amy said. "How could we do that? We can't use the phone in the administration building without permission."

"Well, we'll just have to get permission," Jessica said firmly. But when the girls asked what her plan was, she had to admit she didn't have one.

Elizabeth paced the room for a few minutes. Then she said, "What if Jess and I say we've forgotten our mother's birthday? We could ask to call home and wish her Happy Birthday?"

Jessica's face lit up. "That's a good idea! How could anyone be mean enough to say no to that?"

"Try it," Amy urged. "And you'd better get over to the administration building before the storm gets any worse."

Even with the protection provided by the umbrella Ellen gave them, Elizabeth and Jessica were soaking wet by the time they made it to the shelter of the administration building. The wind was blowing so hard it took the two of them to slam the door shut behind them.

"I'm worried," Elizabeth whispered. "What if Grace is out alone in this horrible weather?"

"Oh, I'm sure she's at the bus station by now," Jessica answered, but her expression was troubled.

The girls had hoped one of the friendlier counselors, or even Mrs. Edwards, would be sitting at the front desk. Instead, they found Tina, looking as stern as usual. "What are you girls doing here?" she barked. "All campers have orders to stay in their bunks while it's raining." She went over to a cabinet and threw them a towel.

Jessica rubbed herself off quickly and handed the towel to Elizabeth. "We need to call our mother."

"Why?" Tina asked suspiciously.

"It's her birthday," Elizabeth chimed in, "and we want to talk to her."

Tina stared at them for what seemed a very long time. "You should have sent a card, but I suppose it's all right. There's a pay phone on the wall down the hall. You can use that one."

"Whew," Jessica said when the twins were out of earshot. "That was close."

The phone was far enough away from the front desk so that Tina couldn't see them looking up the phone number of the bus station in the telephone book that hung on the wall. Nervously, Elizabeth reached into her pocket and pulled out the change she needed for the call.

When someone at the bus station answered the phone, Elizabeth said, "I'm looking for a friend who was taking a bus to Los Angeles. She has red curly hair and her name is Grace."

The stationmaster's voice was brusque. "There hasn't been anyone of that description in here all day."

"Are you sure?" Elizabeth said desperately. "Maybe someone else saw her."

"I've been here since seven A.M., and the only child that's passed through here was a boy of about two or three."

"All right, thanks." Elizabeth slowly hung up the receiver.

"Oh, Lizzie, she didn't make it?"

"No."

Both girls were silent, listening to the storm blowing a large tree branch against the windowpane. Outside it was black as night.

Elizabeth reached over for Jessica's hand. "Now what do we do, Jess?"

Jessica shook her head. "I don't know."

Nine

◇

A crack of thunder suddenly shook the room.

"It's horrible out," Elizabeth said with a shiver. "If Grace is walking around in that—"

"Don't think about it," Jessica implored.

"I can't think about anything else."

"What should we do?"

"We have to tell, Jess. You know we do."

"But we could be in big trouble."

"Us? What about Grace?"

Jessica nodded. "You're right." She looked over at Tina. "But do we have to tell her?"

"No, we'll just ask for Mrs. Edwards." Elizabeth took a deep breath and marched over to the front desk. "Excuse me," she said politely, "we need to see Mrs. Edwards."

"Mrs. Edwards is busy," Tina said, without bothering to look up from her work.

"But it's important," Elizabeth said desperately.

"How so?"

Elizabeth shot Jessica a look that said *Help*!

"Tina, we have to see Mrs. Edwards," Jessica said firmly. "It's a matter of life and death. If you don't let us see her right now, a lot of people are going to be very sorry."

Tina looked at them closely, then she got out of her chair. "I'll get her for you."

"Nice work, Jess," Elizabeth whispered.

Mrs. Edwards smiled as she walked into the room. "Well, well, the Wakefield twins. What can I do for you?"

Neither of the girls knew where to start. Finally, Elizabeth cleared her throat. "It's like this, Mrs. Edwards. Someone is missing."

"One of our campers?" Mrs. Edwards asked with concern.

"Not exactly."

With help from Jessica, Elizabeth quickly told the whole story: about Grace's problem at home, her desire to come to camp, and about how she was staying up at the shack. Then she explained how Grace had played hide-and-seek with the staff, participating in all the camp activities. Every word from Elizabeth's lips made Mrs. Edwards' jaw drop a little further.

Elizabeth finished by saying that Grace had decided to leave because she felt she was becoming a burden. Mrs. Edwards shook her head. "This is really quite unbelievable."

"Oh, it's all true," Jessica assured her.

"That's not what I meant. To think that you could keep an unregistered camper right here, under my nose . . . well, all that is irrelevant for the moment. All that matters is finding Grace. I'll deal with you girls later."

Jessica didn't like the way that sounded, but at least Grace's safety was now in Mrs. Edwards' hands. All they could do now was wait and hope.

"Do you know where I can reach Grace's mother?" Mrs. Edwards asked the twins.

Elizabeth supplied the name of the spa, and Mrs. Edwards picked up the phone. She dismissed the twins with a wave of her hand. "You'd better send Jamie to me. I'll let you know if there's any news."

The storm had blown over, at least temporarily, and only a smattering of rain was still falling when the twins left the administration building.

"That was one of the hardest things I've ever had to do," Elizabeth murmured.

"Me, too," Jessica agreed fervently. "But, Lizzie, why didn't you tell Mrs. Edwards about Barbara's part in all this? You deliberately left it out, didn't you?"

"Barbara took advantage of the situation, but what good would it do to get her into trouble?"

"It's all Barbara's fault that Grace left," Jessica argued. "If we're going to be punished, so should she."

Elizabeth sighed. "She's such a miserable person, she's probably been punished enough."

"How can you say that?" Jessica asked, horrified. "We've all suffered because of her and I don't think she should get away with it. I'm going to ask the others what they think," she said, as she opened the door to their cabin.

All was quiet. The girls were reading, except for Nancy and Amy who were playing checkers at the game table. Barbara seemed to be asleep in her bunk. Jessica was surprised that no one rushed up to ask her about Grace, but then she noticed Jamie sitting in the corner of the cabin.

"Did you make the call to your mother?" Jamie wanted to know.

Elizabeth was sick of all the lying. "We didn't call Mom."

"Why not?" Jamie asked with surprise.

"Mrs. Edwards wants to see you. I guess she'll explain things."

A puzzled Jamie grabbed an umbrella and left the cabin. The second she was gone, everyone ran over to the twins, wanting to know what had happened. Jessica filled them in.

Amy slumped on a chair. "So you still don't know anything about Grace."

"No. And I'm really scared," Elizabeth admitted.

Kelly shook her head. "It sounds like Mrs. Edwards was really upset."

"You can't blame her, can you?" Elizabeth said. "She was very worried about Grace."

"And she couldn't have been very happy with our part in this," Amy added.

"That's for sure."

"You know whose fault this is, don't you?" Jessica asked.

Ellen nodded in Barbara's direction. "Sleeping Beauty. If she really is sleeping."

"I doubt that she is," Jessica said grimly, walking over to Barbara and giving her a shake on the shoulder.

Barbara was up in an instant. It was obvious to everyone she had been awake the whole time.

"I don't know why you're blaming this whole thing on me," she said, brushing the hair out of her eyes.

"Why?" Jessica exploded. "You're the one who kept trying to blackmail everyone. You said you were going to tell on Grace if we didn't do whatever you wanted, and Grace thought she was ruining everyone's good time. What else did you expect her to do?"

Ellen stood next to Jessica. "I can't believe a nice girl like Grace has to leave camp, and we get stuck with you!"

"But we're lucky in one respect," Kimberly said, joining the group surrounding Barbara. "Now that Grace is gone, and everyone knows the truth, we don't have to take any more of Barbara Fields' orders."

"You're right," Jessica cried. "Barbara, your days in this cabin are numbered. You don't have a thing to hold over our heads anymore."

Barbara looked as if she were about to cry.

Jessica turned to the others. "We want her out, don't we, girls?"

Before anyone could answer, Jamie burst into

the room. "I don't believe what Mrs. Edwards just told me."

Most of the girls hung their heads. They all liked Jamie and knew how hurt she must be at finding her campers had deceived her.

Elizabeth tried to explain. "Jamie, Grace was having a terrible time at home. She really needed to be here with friends."

"I'm sure you had your reasons."

"We really did," Elizabeth said.

"We'll have to talk about this later. Right now, the most important thing is finding Grace."

"Have they gotten in touch with her mother yet?" Amy asked.

"Yes. And it's a good thing her spa is only about one hour from here. She's driving right up."

"Has anybody notified the police?" Jessica whispered the last word.

"Of course. They've checked the bus station, but Grace never made it there, as you know. She's not at her godmother's, either."

"That means she could be anywhere," Elizabeth said softly.

"We're starting a search party," Jamie informed them. "There's another storm brewing, but we may be able to do some looking in the general vicinity before it starts raining again."

Efficiently, she divided the girls into two groups, but neither of them wanted Barbara with them.

"Oh, come on," Jamie said impatiently. "Can't you put your petty squabbles aside while we try to locate Grace?"

The girls felt stung by this, and Elizabeth was about to ask Barbara to join their search party, when Barbara ran toward the door, saying, "Never mind, I don't want to go with them. Maybe I'll find her myself."

Before anyone could stop her, Barbara flung the door open and ran outside.

Jessica shook her head. "Boy, is she weird."

Jamie looked at her steadily. "Sometimes when people have problems at home, it comes out in unpleasant behavior."

"What problems at home?"

"We don't have time to talk about that now. After Grace is found, maybe we can sort this whole mess out."

All over camp, girls organized into small groups. They searched through the buildings and around the stable, but then the rain started coming down in buckets and the campers were ordered back to their cabins.

The girls of Bunk Seven had just returned and were drying themselves when Mrs. Edwards appeared at the door. Her face was serious.

"Girls," she said, "I've just been talking to Jamie. She tells me Barbara has run off." Mrs. Edwards looked around the room. "I take it she hasn't returned."

It was true, Barbara was still gone. Now she, too, was out wandering around in the storm.

"I have the feeling I don't know the whole story about what went on with Grace. Was Barbara involved somehow?"

For a few seconds no one said anything. Then Elizabeth spoke up. "You're right, Mrs. Edwards. With Barbara gone too, I guess we'd better tell you everything."

Finally, the cabin was in sight. Climbing up the hill, slipping and sliding in the rain, was an almost impossible job, but Barbara knew she didn't have any choice but to keep going. The storm worsened as she stumbled up the hill, and staying out in the whipping wind and torrents of rain was dangerous.

The last few steps were the hardest. The wetness blurred her vision, and she grabbed wildly at any branch she could to help steady herself. With great effort she pushed the door of the cabin open against the wind.

For a few moments, Barbara just sat on the wooden chair, catching her breath. Then she reached over for a wool blanket lying in a heap next to the cold fireplace and wrapped it around her.

She had never been up here in the rain, but even with the storm pounding outside, it was the same comforting place it always was. Her place. Her secret place. No matter what jibes and jeers she had to put up with from the other campers each day, Barbara knew that she could come up here and escape. Here is where she could come to read her letters. Where she could cry over them without anyone seeing her, or making fun of her.

Barbara waited until she stopped shivering. Then she went to the rickety desk and opened a drawer. She removed a packet of letters addressed to her and went back to the chair. She unfolded the first letter, smoothing the creases in the paper.

DEAR BARBARA,
I HOPE YOU ARE ENJOYING CAMP. I MISS YOU SO MUCH! YOU'RE ALL I THINK ABOUT WHILE THIS DIVORCE IS

GOING ON. YOUR FATHER IS NOT VERY
HELPFUL. SOMETIMES I WONDER IF HE
CARES ABOUT ANYTHING ANYMORE.
HIS ACTIONS DON'T SHOW IT. HE'S
BARELY GOING TO GIVE US ENOUGH
MONEY TO LIVE ON AFTER THE DI-
VORCE. WHEN YOU WRITE HIM, I HOPE
YOU WILL MENTION THIS TO HIM.
MEANWHILE, I HOPE YOU ARE MAKING
LOTS OF NEW FRIENDS. I LOVE YOU.
LOVE, MOMMY.

Lots of friends. What a joke, Barbara thought bitterly.
She pulled a second letter from the packet.

DEAR BARBARA,
HOW'S MY LITTLE GIRL? I'M EXPECTING
SOME LETTERS FROM YOU, BARB, SO
DON'T LET ME DOWN. THINGS ARE ALL
RIGHT AT HOME, BUT YOUR MOTHER IS
BEING STUBBORN AS USUAL. DIVORCE
IS A VERY DIFFICULT THING. I WISH
YOU'D TELL HER TO SIMMER DOWN.
ANYWAY, HAVE A GOOD TIME AT CAMP.
MISS YOU, HONEY.
LOVE, DAD.

Tears formed in Barbara's eyes. Everyday
there were new letters from her parents, each with

the same message. You mom is wrong, your father is wrong. And that left Barbara right in the middle.

Now the tears splashed down Barbara's cheeks. Couldn't they see what they were doing? Barbara hated the whole idea of the divorce. Her family breaking up! But what made it worse was the constant tug-of-war her parents put her through. They were grown-ups, so why couldn't they work things out instead of trying to get her to act as a go-between? And each of them wanted her loyalty. Whose side was she supposed to be on, anyway?

Barbara got up and looked out the window. The rain was still pouring down. In the distance she could see the camp buildings grouped in a circle. Both her parents always wrote they hoped she was having fun at camp. If they only knew the truth. The girls had hated her right from the start. She knew they whispered behind her back because she didn't want to join in all the talk and laughter. Well, maybe she hadn't felt like it with all she had had on her mind. In the very beginning, she had wanted to be alone, but she might have come out of her shell if someone had been nice to her. Instead, they had started silly rumors about her, saying she was mean. But she had showed them. She had been the boss, at least, for a while.

Now that Grace was gone, though, they would have it in for her again.

"I don't care," Barbara muttered to herself. "Someday they're all going to be sorry they've been so mean to me. They're all looking for Grace, but no one cares what happens to me."

Now the tears flowed in earnest, matching the rain that was coursing down the window. A crack of thunder shook the cabin, and suddenly Barbara was scared. *Could this shack withstand the storm?* she wondered. The journey up there had been treacherous, but maybe it would be better to try and get back to camp, although the prospect was hardly tempting.

Sniffling, Barbara tried to collect her thoughts so she would know the right thing to do. Then she heard a noise coming from the back room.

Barbara could feel her heart pounding. "Who's that?" she called in a shaky voice.

When there was no answer, she moved closer to the door. "Is anybody there?"

A figure appeared in the doorway. "Barbara?"

Barbara's eyes grew wide. "Grace! What are you doing here?"

Ten

◇

Grace limped into the room, her face pale. "I twisted my ankle. I was taking a nap in the other room when the thunder woke me up."

"Do you know everyone is worried sick about you?" Barbara demanded.

"Why?" Grace sat heavily on the wooden chair. "Don't they think I'm at my godmother's?"

"No, they don't. Elizabeth called the bus station and was told that you never made it. She had to tell Mrs. Edwards the truth and now the whole camp is looking for you."

"You mean she told her I've been hiding out since camp started?"

"Yes. And don't think Mrs. Edwards wasn't mad."

Grace shook her head. "What a mess. And I thought leaving would save everyone lots of trouble."

"What happened?" Barbara demanded. "How come you didn't go to your godmother's?"

Settling herself in a more comfortable position, Grace said, "I left for the bus station early this morning. I knew it was going to be a long walk, but I hadn't counted on the rain. I was only a quarter of the way there, when I could see the storm coming up, so I decided to turn back. By the time I started climbing the hill, it was slippery, and I fell and hurt my ankle. I had a hard time making it up here into the cabin. Eventually, I fell asleep."

"And I suppose you think this is all my fault," Barbara bristled.

"Not really."

"That's what everybody else thinks," Barbara said accusingly. "Your note practically said the reason you were going was because of me."

"I was upset, especially after you won the trophy for my sculpture," Grace admitted. "But now I see things a little differently."

Barbara paced the room. "For your information, I didn't enter your horse in the arts-and-crafts contest just to be mean."

"You didn't?"

"No. Jessica never gave me a chance to tell you, but I thought you deserved the trophy, and I figured the only way you would get it was if I entered it in my name. And I was right; you did win first prize."

"You did that for me?" Grace asked.

Barbara's tone was curt. "Yes. When we get back to camp, I'll give you the trophy."

"Oh, Barbara, that was a really kind thing to do."

Barbara stopped and looked at Grace suspiciously. "How come you're being so nice to me all of a sudden?"

"Well, I think I understand you better now."

This made Barbara feel good. No matter how it appeared, she had always liked Grace. As soon as she'd heard that Grace had family problems, Barbara had felt they had something in common. "You know, I was the one who gave the twins your letter this morning. I didn't even read it."

"I thought they'd come up here and find it. By then I would have disappeared. Now, everything's a mess."

"I'm going to be in trouble, too," Barbara said glumly.

"You know, Barbara," Grace said hesitantly, "I realize why you acted the way you did."

"You do?"

Grace nodded. "I found your letters."

Barbara could feel her heart pounding. "My letters?"

"Yes."

"When did you find them?" Barbara demanded.

"Today. My ankle was beginning to swell up, so I started looking for something to wrap around it. I checked the drawers and that's when I found them."

"And you read them." The thought made Barbara feel ill.

"At first I didn't realize you were the Barbara in the letters, but then I remembered how you always disappeared during the day, and I figured you probably brought them up here to read."

Barbara ran over to the chair and stuffed the letters into her pocket. "These are my personal property!" she yelled. "You had no right to read them."

"I told you I found them by accident."

Barbara was near tears. "But they were personal."

Grace limped toward Barbara. Her ankle had swollen to twice its normal size. "Look, nobody knows better than I do how terrible it is when your parents fight."

"Are your parents divorced?" Barbara challenged her.

"No," Grace admitted, "but I know how it is to be caught in the middle."

The tears started falling down Barbara's face. "You're going to tell everyone, aren't you? You're going to tell all your friends that I came up here and cried every day."

"Barbara . . ."

"Well, forget it, you're not going to have the chance. Maybe you can't get away from this horrible place, but I will."

Grace was frightened by the distraught look on Barbara's face.

"There's a gigantic storm going on, Barbara. You'd better not go anywhere right now."

"You can't give me orders," Barbara yelled. "I wouldn't stay another minute in this cabin with a little sneak like you."

Barbara rushed to the door. Opening it

against the wind took all her strength, but she pushed it open and ran out into the middle of the gale.

The wind whipped against her and the rain felt like pellets hitting her face. Barbara looked around, trying to see the best way down the hill, but the rain had turned the ground to mud and her steps were slowed as she tried to maneuver through the thick sludge.

A crack of lightning broke through the dark sky, illuminating Barbara's path for a few seconds. She tried to orient herself and thought she saw the direction that would take her safely down the hill. Then she heard an intense crackling sound behind her.

Barbara turned and a horrifying sight met her eyes. The roof of the shack was lined with fire. Lightning had struck the building and now flames leaped around the shack. Barbara stood stock-still as she watched pieces of burning roof fall inside the shack where Grace was stranded.

"Oh, no," she moaned.

Barbara wanted to continue running down the hill. Surely Grace would be able to get herself out. Then Barbara remembered the condition of Grace's ankle. For a few heart-stopping seconds,

Barbara watched the door. When Grace did not appear, Barbara flew back to the shack and flung open the door.

The cabin was filled with smoke, but bits of burning wood brightened the darkness, giving enough light for Barbara to make out Grace's body lying in the corner of the room.

"Grace!" Barbara screamed, but the injured girl did not move.

Barbara moved toward her, narrowly avoiding being hit by a piece of smoldering wood from the roof. When she reached Grace, she shook her, but got no response.

"Grace, we have to get out of here!" Barbara's plea was punctuated by the sound of burning wood falling all around them.

Grace moved a little as Barbara tried to prop her up. As soon as she lifted her head, Grace started coughing, but Barbara wouldn't let her catch her breath.

"Come on, there's no time for that. We have to go."

Grace looked around her, bewildered. "What's happening?" she cried, her eyes widening in disbelief.

"Lightning hit the shack," Barbara muttered, using all her strength to lift Grace to her feet.

"My ankle," Grace moaned, as she stood up.

"Lean on me." Barbara draped Grace's arm over her shoulder and steadied her on her feet.

Grace's cough worsened, but Barbara would not allow her to rest. Half pulling, half pushing, she forced the two of them to the doorway. Once they got outside into the cool air, they were safe.

It wasn't raining as hard now and the strong wind had died down to a steady breeze. Barbara helped Grace to a small pine tree and sat her down.

"Are you all right?" she asked.

Grace nodded, still coughing.

"I'm going to go back to the camp for help."

Grace grabbed Barbara's hand. "Don't leave me," she cried.

"Grace, I have to go. I'll never be able to get you down the hill by myself, not in your condition."

Grace looked at Barbara. "You saved my life."

"It wasn't anything," Barbara muttered with embarrassment.

"What are you talking about? You didn't have to come back, but you did."

Barbara shook her head.

"You were furious with me, but when I really

needed help, you risked your life for me," Grace said, her voice full of admiration.

"Anyone would have done the same thing."

"No, they wouldn't have," Grace declared. "Most people would have been too scared. Barbara, I'll never forget what you did."

Barbara turned her head. "What's that noise?" she asked sharply.

Grace peered over her shoulder. "I hear it, but I can't see anything."

Barbara got up and walked to the edge of the hilltop. "Oh, thank goodness. There's a search party coming up here. Mrs. Edwards, and Tina, and a woman I don't know."

Grace leaned back against the tree, exhausted. "Then we're going to be all right."

Quicker than Barbara would have thought possible, the rescuers had reached the top of the hill. The woman screamed when she saw the charred cabin.

"Oh, no. My poor Grace! Is she in there?"

"Mother, over here," Grace cried.

"Grace!" Mrs. Oliver ran to the tree with Mrs. Edwards and Tina right behind her. Mrs. Oliver gathered Grace in her arms, murmuring to her.

"Oh, Mom." Now Grace began to cry.

Mrs. Edwards surveyed the situation. "Are you all right?" she asked.

"I think so," Grace choked out a sob.

"Tina," Mrs. Edwards ordered, "go down and get the first aid kit. And call the paramedics. It may take them a while to get here on these muddy roads, but she may need oxygen."

"No, I'm all right," Grace protested.

Mrs. Oliver stroked her daughter's hair. "Don't be silly. We want the doctors to look at you right away."

Mrs. Edwards nodded at Tina who took off down the hill as quickly as conditions would allow.

"What about Barbara? Will they look at her, too?"

Mrs. Oliver glanced around. "Who is Barbara, dear?"

"Barbara's the girl who saved me."

Mrs. Edwards was also perplexed. "I don't understand; she was here just a second ago."

"She saved you?" Mrs. Oliver asked her daughter.

"Oh, yes, Mom. I must have fainted from the smoke, and she helped me out of the cabin."

"We'll find her, don't worry," Mrs. Oliver said. "I have to thank her for saving my little girl's life." She gave Grace another hug.

Grace looked around her. "But where could she have gone?"

"I don't know," Mrs. Edwards said grimly. "If she doesn't turn up by the time we get you taken care of, we may have to send out a search party for Barbara."

The next half hour was filled with confusion. Tina came back up the hill with the news that the paramedics would be there as soon as possible. She added that the camp had gotten in touch with Mr. Oliver and he was on his way as well.

"He's going to be very angry at me, isn't he?" Grace whispered between coughs.

"Let's not think about that right now," Mrs. Oliver responded. "The most important thing is having you checked out by the paramedics and making sure that you're all right."

The paramedics arrived with all of their equipment. Although Grace was feeling better by now, they examined her thoroughly, making sure that the smoke she had inhaled had done no damage to her lungs. Then they looked at her ankle and taped it properly so it would heal.

"Her ankle isn't broken, is it?" Mrs. Oliver asked anxiously.

"No, ma'am. I'm sure Grace is going to be just fine," the young paramedic said with a smile. "But just to be sure, we're going to put her on a stretcher to bring her back to camp. She'd have a hard time navigating this hill right now."

It was an odd procession that made its way down Crying Moon Mountain to Camp Loconda. Grace, feeling a bit like a princess, was lying on the stretcher, carried down by the two paramedics. Mrs. Oliver held her hand all the way, while Tina and Mrs. Edwards followed behind.

Most of the campers inside their cabins were peering out their windows, trying to get a look at what was happening. Mrs. Edwards directed the paramedics to her office, where Grace had a surprise waiting. There, pacing the floor, was her father.

"Gracie!" he cried, coming over to give her a hug. The paramedics helped her off the stretcher and placed her carefully in Mrs. Edwards' big leather chair.

"I think these people need a few moments by themselves right now," Mrs. Edwards declared, ushering everyone out.

"Is she all right?" Mr. Oliver asked, looking at his wife with concern.

She nodded. "She'll be limping for a while, but she'll survive."

"Thank goodness!"

"If you could have seen that burnt shack," Mrs. Oliver said with a shudder. "This could have been a tragedy."

"It would have been a tragedy without Barbara Fields," Grace said soberly. "She's the girl who saved me, Daddy."

Mr. Oliver kneeled down in front of his daughter and clasped her hands in his. "I don't understand how you got here, Grace. I couldn't believe it when I got a call at the fishing lodge saying you had been injured at Camp Loconda."

Grace looked down, saying nothing.

"I think it's time you explained things to us," her mother said gently.

In as few words as possible, Grace explained how she had gotten to the camp and how she had been hidden by her friends.

"I talked to Kay," Mr. Oliver informed his wife. "When she heard the message on her machine, she just assumed that we had changed our plans. It never occurred to her to check."

"I called to talk to Grace while I was at the spa, but there was never any answer. I thought you were having too much fun to think of calling me," Mrs. Oliver told her daughter.

"Kay said when Grace didn't come, she went

out of town and got back just this morning," Mr. Oliver reported.

"That explains why she never returned my messages."

"When she listened to her answering machine this morning, she was really upset." Mr. Oliver turned back to his daughter. "But, honey, I still don't understand. Why did you just run off like that?"

"Because I wanted to go to camp," Grace said, her head hanging down. "Everyone said how great it was going to be, and I didn't want to miss all the fun."

"Originally, we talked about you going," Mrs. Oliver said thoughtfully, "but when we changed the plan, you didn't say much about it. You certainly didn't make a fuss."

"I was afraid," Grace whispered.

"Afraid?" Her father frowned. "Afraid of what?"

"You two were arguing so much. I was afraid if I mentioned camp, you'd have another reason for a fight."

Mr. and Mrs. Oliver exchanged glances, their distress written clearly on their faces.

"I guess we were fighting a great deal," Mrs. Oliver admitted.

"This has been a painful time," Mr. Oliver agreed, his voice soft.

"I just wanted the fighting to stop." Grace burst into tears. "I couldn't stand it."

Both Grace's parents went to comfort her.

"Please, don't cry," Mrs. Oliver said, stroking her daughter's red curls. "It's over now."

"Try to calm down," Mr. Oliver murmured.

Grace sobbed into her father's handkerchief, until she got control of herself.

"Sorry," she sniffled.

"Don't be sorry. I think your mother and I both see how upsetting the last few months have been for you, now."

"They have been," Grace said, wiping her eyes with the back of her hand. "I wish you weren't getting a divorce."

Mr. Oliver walked over to the window. "Grace, I'm not going to lie to you. I don't think either your mother or I have come to a decision about our marriage."

Mrs. Oliver shook her head. "Your father is right. This is going to take more serious thinking on both of our parts. But I know one decision I've come to, and I'm sure your father will agree. This bickering has just got to stop."

"You're right," said Mr. Oliver. "We've been

so concerned about our own feelings and emotions that we haven't given enough thought to how you were coping with things, Grace."

Mrs. Oliver gave her daughter a kiss. "Whatever happens, we both love you very much, Grace, and from now on we're going to take your feelings into consideration, as well."

Grace broke into a trembling smile. "That would mean a lot to me, Mom, Dad."

"That's decided, then," Mr. Oliver said in a hearty voice.

"We do have one more decision to make," Mrs. Oliver said. "Shall we all go back to Sweet Valley or continue on with our separate vacations?"

Her father gave a little bow. "Grace, may we hear your ideas on this matter?" he asked in a very formal tone.

Grace giggled. "Well, since you're asking me, I'd like to finish out the week at camp. This time I'd like to stay as a regular camper. One that everybody knows is here."

Mr. and Mrs. Oliver looked at each other and nodded. "I think that can be arranged," her mother said.

Her father came over and shook her hand. "Let me be the first to welcome Camp Loconda's newest member!"

Eleven

◆

The girls of Bunk Seven peered out the window that faced the center of the camp.

"Can you see anything?" Jessica demanded, trying to look over Kelly's shoulder.

"No," Elizabeth replied. "There's still nothing happening outside the administration building."

Nancy moved away from her place at the window and flopped down on her bed. "We've been looking outside that window for twenty minutes and we haven't seen a thing since Grace was carried in."

"At least the ambulance left," Amy commented as she continued her watch.

"Jamie did come in to tell us that Grace is all

right, except for a sprained ankle," Elizabeth added.

"But she hurried away before she could tell us much else," Jessica grumbled.

Elizabeth turned away and joined Nancy on her bed. "Grace must have been hiding up at the shack. They brought her down from that direction."

"We probably just missed her when we went up there," Jessica said. "She must have come back right after we left."

Kelly made a face. "This never would have happened if it wasn't for Barbara."

"You're right," Ellen agreed. "It was all because of Barbara and her stupid threats."

"I hope she's feeling miserable about it," Kimberly put in.

Jessica sat down at the game table. "All she knows is that Grace is gone. She doesn't know that she's been injured."

"I wonder where she is," Nancy said.

Elizabeth looked thoughtful. "So do I."

"When she does get back, I've got a few things I want to say to her. We never finished our conversation," Jessica said with foreboding in her voice.

"You're going to have your chance." Kelly

turned away from the window and faced the girls. "Here she comes."

The room was silent when Barbara entered. She hadn't wanted to come back to the bunk, but since she had faded away from the scene on the hilltop, she had walked until she was exhausted. There were so many things to think about, the shock of the fire and the rescue, as well as the fact that Grace knew about her letters and her situation at home.

All her walking and thinking hadn't done her much good, however. She was still as upset as ever and so tired that all she wanted to do was fall into bed. She had hoped her bunkmates would be gone, but they were all there: a very unfriendly welcoming committee. Barbara didn't say a word to anyone. She just walked over to her bunk and lay down on the bed.

But Jessica wasn't about to let her off that easily. She marched over to Barbara's bunk, her arms folded in front of her. "Do you know what happened today?" she asked, practically spitting out the words.

Barbara sighed and sat up. "Yes. Grace ran away."

"Ran away and hurt her foot!"

Barbara could tell that Jessica didn't know about the fire in the shack.

"She's all right," Barbara said wearily.

"A lot you care," Nancy called from her bed. "You're the one responsible for her leaving."

Barbara felt her anger welling up. "You all think you're so smart. You don't know half of what went on up at the shack."

"We don't want to know, either," Jessica said hotly.

Ellen marched over and joined Jessica, her face set in the same forbidding expression. "We know what happened down here."

"And we don't like it," Kimberly said joining her friends.

"So what are you going to do about it?" Barbara asked threateningly.

"We've already told Mrs. Edwards what's been going on around here," Jessica said. "And next we're going to tell her how you stole Grace's horse and put it in the show."

"You've got a lot to worry about, Barbara," Ellen said with satisfaction.

For the first time, fear crept into Barbara's face. Her parents would be horrified if she was kicked out of camp. What was worse, each parent would wind up blaming the other for her bad behavior, and another horrendous round of name-calling would begin.

Barbara got off her bed and faced her accusers. "Look, maybe I didn't handle things the right way."

"The right way?" Jessica hooted. "You've been a super pain around here for days."

Ellen nodded. "And now that the secret about Grace is out, we don't have to put up with you."

Before Barbara could answer, Jamie popped her head into the cabin. "Girls, good news. Grace is going to be staying at camp. Her parents have arranged it with Mrs. Edwards."

Bunk Seven began cheering, but Barbara remained silent. If Grace stayed, would she tell any of Barbara's secrets?

"Would you like to go see Grace?" Jamie asked.

A chorus of approval answered Jamie's question. The girls hurried out the door. Only Barbara and Jessica remained where they were.

"Aren't you coming?" Elizabeth asked, turning back to her sister.

Jessica shook her head. "Not now. I'll see Grace in a little while."

Elizabeth looked at the hard expressions on the faces of Barbara and Jessica. "Are you sure?"

"Yes," Jessica replied curtly.

The cabin was empty. "So what now, Jessica?" Barbara asked with trepidation.

"Now, I'm going to make sure you go home."

"How are you going to do that?"

"I'm going to start by packing you up." Jessica marched over to Barbara's duffel bag, picked it up, and threw it outside the cabin.

"Hey, what are you doing?" Barbara looked alarmed.

"Getting rid of you." Jessica took the books that Barbara had stowed under the bed and tossed them outside as well.

Barbara was too stunned to move. She watched in disbelief as Jessica picked up her possessions, one by one, and hauled them outside. Finally, she sprang into action. "Hey, quit it!"

"No way!" Jessica yelled. "Nobody in this bunk wants you here, Barbara, and if we can't get you to leave camp, at least you won't be in Bunk Seven anymore."

Barbara was near tears. How humiliating to have her things tossed outside as if they were garbage. She swallowed her pride. "Please, Jessica, bring everything back inside."

Jessica stood her ground. "No. You've been nothing but trouble to us. Why, you caused Grace's accident! There's no way you're staying in this bunk."

Barbara went outside, picked up a few of her belongings, and tried to bring them back to the cabin, but Jessica barred her way.

The two were frozen face to face when they heard the noisy chatter of their bunkmates.

Grace, leaning on a cane that had been found in the infirmary, was surrounded by her friends. Although they were moving slowly because of Grace's ankle, the girls were laughing and giggling as they discussed all the fun that they would be having in the remaining days of camp.

When they got close enough to see Barbara's things spread all over the grass, the group stopped in amazement. Elizabeth was the first to find her voice. "What's going on here?"

Jessica remained cool. Tossing her hair over her shoulder, she spoke directly to Grace. "How do you like the new place I've chosen for Barbara's things?"

Grace's face grew as red as her curls. "I don't like it at all."

"You don't?" Jessica asked, confused.

"Of course not." She looked at the clothes,

books, and stationery spread everywhere. "What a mean thing to do."

"Maybe you don't understand, Grace. I'm making sure that Barbara leaves the cabin. That way you can have her bed."

Grace hobbled over to Jessica. "I think you're the one who doesn't understand. Barbara saved my life."

Jessica's eyes grew round. "What are you talking about?"

"I was up in the shack with a sprained ankle, when lightning hit the building and a fire broke out."

"You're kidding!"

"No, I'm not. The smoke from the fire made me pass out and if Barbara hadn't rescued me, I would have died up there."

Jessica turned to Barbara in amazement. "You didn't tell us any of that."

In a shaky voice, Barbara said, "You wouldn't have believed me even if I did."

Jessica, feeling secretly ashamed, realized that was probably true. "You still pulled a lot of mean tricks," she reminded Barbara.

"Barbara had her reasons," Grace said before Barbara could respond.

Afraid that Grace might spell out those reasons, Barbara looked at the assembled group and said, "Never mind why I did those things. Maybe Jessica is right and I don't belong here."

Before anyone could stop her, Barbara ran toward the stable. She pushed open the doors and slammed them behind her, taking deep breaths as she leaned against the heavy wooden slats. Finally, she calmed down a little. After all the commotion, it felt good to be in a dark, comforting place, with only an occasional neigh from one of the horses to break the silence.

Barbara found Brownie's stall and went inside. She gave the large, brown horse a few pats as she wiped the tears away from her face. Brownie looked at her with gentle eyes. *Did he know she was in trouble?*

The stable door opened. Barbara tried to duck down behind Brownie, but it was too late. Grace saw her through the shadows.

"Barbara, I've got to talk to you."

"Go away, Grace."

"Barbara, please," Grace urged.

Reluctantly, Barbara came out of Brownie's stall. "What do you want?"

"Why don't we sit down on that bench?" Grace said, pointing to the side. "My ankle is killing me."

When they were settled, Barbara, her expression stony, said, "I don't know what you have to say to me."

"First I want to thank you for saving my life."

"You already did that."

"And I want to apologize for what Jessica did."

Barbara sighed. "You don't have to get involved with that."

Grace looked shocked. "You don't think I would just abandon a friend, do you?" she wanted to know.

"A . . . friend?"

"Of course I think of you as my friend. You were thinking of me when you entered my statue in the contest."

"I always liked you, Grace," Barbara said shyly. "Even though it may not have seemed that way."

"You were upset because I found your letters, Barbara, but it made me feel closer to you and I began to understand why you had done some of those things."

"I couldn't seem to make any friends. Everyone just talked about me and made up stupid lies," Barbara said, her head down.

"I know," Grace said quietly.

"And I was jealous that everyone liked you so much. For a while bossing everyone around made me feel powerful, but the truth is, I was wishing I could find a way to stop it."

"Well, it's all over now," Grace said cheerfully. "You can start over with a clean slate."

Barbara shook her head. "The girls will never forgive me."

"I think they've already started to since they found out you saved my life."

"But Jessica and some of the others—"

"You'll have to convince them," Grace interrupted. "And to do that you should be honest about your problems."

"You mean, tell them about my family?" Barbara asked with a quaver in her voice.

"It's not a crime to have trouble at home. Lots of girls do; I know I do. They would understand."

"I don't know. What if they laugh at me?"

"They won't, not with me standing right behind you."

"You'd do that?"

"It's the least I can do. Besides, if you don't work things out with the girls, I'll just pick up and go home myself."

Barbara's eyes grew wide. "You wouldn't."

"I certainly would," Grace said stoutly. "And then my vacation would be ruined."

"But that's . . ."

"Blackmail," Grace finished for her. "So now you've got to do what I say. Be honest and be nice. And I insist that you have a good time at camp."

There was a mischievous glint in Grace's eye.

Now Barbara started to see the humor in the situation. "I guess I'm going to be getting a taste of my own medicine."

"You certainly are," Grace said with a laugh.

Jessica surveyed the scene with satisfaction. Paper lanterns decorated the campsite and a local band was setting up near a grove of pine trees.

"This dance is going to be terrific," Jessica told Ellen. "Wait until Lila hears about this."

"By the way," Ellen answered, "I forgot to tell you, Lila isn't having that much fun in Paris."

"So I heard," Jessica said.

"You got a letter from her, too?"

Jessica nodded. "She says she has sore feet."

"I know. Her grandmother has dragged her around to a million museums and she hasn't met one boy."

"Well, we're going to be meeting some boys tonight." Jessica glanced at her watch. "They should be here any minute."

Elizabeth and Amy joined Jessica and Ellen. "I've got to hand it to you, Jess," Elizabeth said. "You said you were going to pull this dance off and you certainly did."

"I was afraid it might not happen," Jessica confessed. "I thought Mrs. Edwards might cancel it as punishment for hiding Grace."

"We got off easy," Amy said. "Only a lecture from Mrs. Edwards."

"Don't forget having to clean up the camp, inside and out," Elizabeth reminded her.

"The cleaning wasn't too bad," Amy said. "Especially since everyone in the camp had to do their part."

Ellen shrugged. "Well, like Mrs. Edwards said, we were all responsible."

"Still, it could have been worse than just a lecture and cleaning up," Elizabeth said.

"Much worse," Jessica agreed fervently. "I would have died if I had to tell the boys there was no dance."

"That's all behind you," her sister said, pointing toward the driveway. "Here come the boys."

*   *   *

The next two hours flew by. The boys came into the campfire area, rather shyly at first, but soon everyone was mingling and the laughing and joking began.

Sandy, his hair slicked back, looking nice in a fresh T-shirt and jeans, came up to Jessica.

"Since we passed the petition around, I think we should start off the dancing," he said.

Jessica brushed the hair out of her eyes. "That sounds great."

Sandy led her out to the makeshift dance floor and started twirling her around. He was a great dancer who knew all the latest steps. Soon the others gathered around them in a circle and clapped their hands in time to the music.

"All right!" someone called.

"They sure can dance," one of the girls said.

Jessica was in heaven. Here she was, the center of attention, dancing with a cute boy. It didn't take much to imagine herself back in Sweet Valley describing the whole scene to Lila. She could hardly wait.

The party was well planned. There was dancing, games, more dancing and then the cook served a fried chicken dinner in the dining room. All the boys agreed that the food was much better at Camp Loconda than at Camp Running Bear.

Elizabeth took her tray and found a seat near Grace and Barbara.

"Do you want to save a seat for Jessica?" Grace asked.

Elizabeth shook her head. "She's got plans for supper."

"Sandy?"

"Who else?" Elizabeth laughed.

"That Jessica."

Elizabeth turned to Barbara. "Are you having fun?"

"She certainly is," Grace answered for her. "Jessica isn't the only one who's attracting attention."

Barbara blushed.

"Who's her new friend?" Elizabeth wanted to know.

Grace pointed toward a figure at the end of the line. "Jerry McAllister."

"Jerry! He's never shown any interest in girls before. Barbara, what's your secret?"

Barbara laughed with embarrassment. "Come on, stop teasing me."

"You know, Barbara, you've really changed," Elizabeth said seriously. "I wouldn't have thought it a week ago, but I really think of you as a friend."

"Thanks, Elizabeth," Barbara said sincerely.

"It took a lot of courage for you to come and tell us about your parents' divorce."

It had been difficult. After their talk in the stable, she and Grace had gone back to Bunk Seven where the girls had had a long, heart-to-heart talk. With Grace's encouragement, Barbara had told the girls how unhappy her home situation was, and how much she wanted to feel important and powerful.

As Grace had predicted, the girls had been supportive. "It could have been different, Barbara, if only we had known," Jessica had said. And now things *were* different.

"Telling you guys was the best decision I could have made," Barbara said with a grin. "Of course, I had a little help."

"I've been giving Barbara all sorts of orders," Grace informed Elizabeth.

"Oh, really?"

"And I have one to give her right now."

Barbara waited expectantly. "I'm listening."

"Let's get out there and make our last night at camp the best one ever!"

We hope you enjoyed reading this book. All the titles currently available in the Sweet Valley Twins series are listed at the front of the book. They are all available at your local bookshop or newsagent, though should you find any difficulty in obtaining the books you would like, you can order direct from the publisher, at the address below. Also, if you would like to know more about the series, or would simply like to tell us what you think of the series, write to:

Kim Prior,
Sweet Valley Twins,
Transworld Publishers Ltd.,
61–63 Uxbridge Road,
Ealing,
London W5 5SA.

To order books, please list the title(s) you would like, and send together with a cheque or postal order made payable to TRANSWORLD PUBLISHERS LTD. Please allow the cost of the book(s) plus postage and packing charges as follows:

All orders up to a total of £5.00   50p
All orders in excess of £5.00   Free

Please note that payment must be made in pounds sterling; other currencies are unacceptable.

(The above applies to readers in the UK and Republic of Ireland only)

If you live in Australia or New Zealand and would like more information about the series, please write to:

Sally Porter,
Sweet Valley Twins,
Transworld Publishers (Aust) Pty. Ltd,.
15–23 Helles Avenue,
Moorebank,
N.S.W. 2170,
AUSTRALIA

Kiri Martin
Sweet Valley Twins,
c/o Corgi and Bantam Books New Zealand,
Cnr. Moselle and Waipareira Avenues,
Henderson,
Auckland,
NEW ZEALAND